Dec 17, 2020

Maame
(MOTHER)

ELIZABETH ALLUA VAAH

MAWENZI
HOUSE

We acknowledge the support of the Canada Council for the Arts for our publishing program. We also acknowledge support from the Government of Ontario through the Ontario Arts Council, and the support of the Government of Canada through the Canada Book Fund.

Cover design by Angelina Vaah
Cover Image by Annie Spratt on Unsplash

Library and Archives Canada Cataloguing in Publication

Title: Maame (Mother) / Elizabeth Allua Vaah.
Names: Vaah, Elizabeth Allua, 1971- author.
Identifiers: Canadiana (print) 20200342983 | Canadiana (ebook) 20200343211 | ISBN 9781774150290
   (softcover) | ISBN 9781774150306 (EPUB) | ISBN 9781774150313 (PDF)
Subjects: LCGFT: Short stories.
Classification: LCC PS8643.A24 M33 2020 | DDC C813/.6—dc23

Printed and bound in Canada by Coach House Printing

Mawenzi House Publishers Ltd.
39 Woburn Avenue (B)
Toronto, Ontario M5M 1K5
Canada
www.mawenzihouse.com

To all mothers, those who choose to be mothers, and those who are chosen by motherhood.

For everything you do, including your many sacrifices.

Contents

Preface

LIFE IN A SMALL WEST African village is a constant rotation between the natural and the supernatural. For girls there is very little time between childhood and adulthood. Within this short window they must learn to navigate a stringent code of conduct if they are to succeed.

What is success? What makes a good mother? What happens when they have eventually had enough? Will this natural-supernatural push-pull give them a chance to find themselves? In *Maame*, we meet Ahu, a young woman married at fifteen and widowed with two children at eighteen, who overcomes all odds to set an example that will inspire future generations of girls from her lineage to reach beyond the limits imposed upon them. In her story, Ahu describes her community, the beliefs and customs that swallow up many of her compatriots, and the self-awareness that brings about her rebellion and freedom.

In the women of *Maame* we see resilience, enterprise, love, selflessness, conflict, heartache, and triumph. Their circumstances may be specific to a time and place, but they reflect what many women everywhere deal with all the time.

Ahu

MY NAME IS AHU. THIS WAS NOT the name I was given at birth. Like all girls and boys in my community, I had a name that matched my gender and day of birth. As a girl born on Friday, I was called Afiba. If I had been a boy I would be called Kofi. I have another name, based on my birth order. As the fifth child of my mother, I am also called Anlunli. Nobody calls me by any of these names anymore, except those who are very close to me, and only on special occasions, when they want to show that they truly belong to my inner circle.

I am told that my father had to wait until I was six months old before naming me after his aunt, Mame Ahu, because it was not uncommon for babies to die at birth or soon after. Perhaps giving newborn babies a generic name was my people's way of not becoming too attached to them, in case they died early. Childbirth in my community is not an easy matter. That is why new mothers are kept indoors, until they are ready, when they are brought out with great fanfare.

These and other thoughts flood through my head as I lie in this makeshift enclosure of raffia sticks and thatch. This multipurpose family bathroom serves as the delivery room today. The two women guiding my baby out into the world are speaking to each other in hushed tones. I can sense the fear in their eyes, as I lie on the raffia mat on the floor. What could be going on? If I focus well enough I should be able to see the other women running about helter-skelter in the yard. I love these enclosures of raffia sticks and thatch because they allow air to flow in freely—a real relief in this tropical, steamy hot weather—and they also allow one to peep out and hear everything that's going on. They did hang cloth curtains on the walls to ensure my privacy, but that's least on my mind. Who cares about privacy when I am going through intense pain with every contraction?

At twenty-four, this is my fourth pregnancy. I hadn't expected the delivery to be so difficult; my other three pregnancies were fairly easy, at least by the standards of what can happen to a pregnant woman in our village.

Aakonu, a village of about five hundred inhabitants, is the last major settlement on the Amanzule River just before it enters the Gulf of Guinea, at the southwestern tip of Ghana. We refer to it as our holy village because it is the only one in the entire community that has visitors and locals alike "washing their feet" before they enter or leave it. This means that visitors have to wade through the two hundred metres of shallow water where the river meets the shoreline, to get to the canoe which will take them to or from the village. There is no pier to walk on, and many first-time visitors to Aakonu express dismay at having to remove their shoes, and sometimes, when we have high tide, even their clothing, in order to get to the canoe. Thick green mangrove borders both ends of the river, making it impossible for anyone to be seen unless they wade through the water to get to the main dock, where the canoe is tethered. The shadow the mangrove casts on the river gives it a darkish green colour. It is no surprise the people believe the god of the river is a tall, handsome man with green eyes, thick, black hair, and smooth jet-black skin.

One thing to note is that nobody is in charge of ferrying people from one end of the river to the other. The entire process runs itself. That means that if a traveller gets to the dock on the south end of the river and the canoe is at the north end, they have to sit down and wait until someone shows up at the north end and brings the canoe over to the south end. One can easily spend several hours waiting, and I have had my fair share of it.

Aakonu village itself is about five hundred metres away after one gets down from the canoe. The walkway from the dock to the village is lined on both sides with coconut trees. To the left one can see the beautiful sandy beach and the sea in the distance. The village has three streets, none of them with a name. The street to the left is bordered by the beach and a row of compounds with multiple huts. Some compounds, like that of Priestess Yaba, have walls of raffia all around them, while others are open. The main street, in the centre, leads to the village square, where the communal well is located. The square is also the main market place. Every morning food vendors congregate there to sell the various foodstuffs they have prepared overnight. Other vendors come from Kamunu, Bokabo and neighbouring landlocked villages to bring cassava, plantain, cocoyam, fruits and vegetables. At the end of that street is the chief's palace, the Catholic Church, and the more recent Catholic Primary School. The third street borders the mangrove that graces the Amanzule River on its way to the sea. There is a smaller communal well on this street as well. However, nobody uses the water from this well for anything other than cleaning. It is said that the Amanzule god did not like it when it was dug, because he thought the people would no longer fetch water from the river if they had more wells. He brought up so much mud that the diggers had to abandon it. Today, although the well stands, its water is so turbid that it is only used for cleaning.

Opanin Nda's compound, where we live, is the first anyone sees when entering the village from the riverside. Opanin Nda was Nana's father. The compound has five main huts, one for Nana and her children, the others for Opanin Nda's single and recently widowed daughters and their children and grandchildren. These huts are for sleeping. On the southern part of the same compound are Nana's kitchen and the other communal kitchen for the rest of Opanin Nda's household. Beside Nana's kitchen is the roofless square enclosure made of raffia and thatch that serves as the bathroom on regular days, a delivery bed for the pregnant women in the household when they go into labour and a mortuary for keeping family members who pass away overnight before they are prepared for burial. There is a gazebo in the middle of the compound where visitors to the home are received. The extra space between the gazebo and the kitchen serves as the playground for the younger members of the household.

Aakonu has a compelling history. Legend has it that a long time ago this was where the last major fight between our tribe, known as the Nzema, and the Nona, a warrior tribe, ended. The Nona were advancing westward, having conquered all the tribes that lay in their path. When they reached Aakonu the chief summoned his elders and other villagers to do whatever they could to repel the Nona. The fishermen lay traps along the river all the way to the sea. The traps were cleverly camouflaged. As the Nona advanced towards the village, they were met by the small but determined army of Aakonu, who hid inside the thick mangrove and fired at the invaders. When the marauding Nona, who were from the hinterland and had never seen the sea before, found that they were trapped by the river on one side and the sea on the other, they abandoned their attack and retreated. Two huge metal pieces, said to be remnants of the guns that were used in that battle, now adorn the entrance to the chief's palace.

I did not meet my biological mother. She died while giving birth to me, the last of five children. Her elder sister, whom everyone, including my siblings and me, called Nana, took care of us. There was no formal adoption, no paperwork to be completed.

In our community Nana was expected to step in and care for "her children." The notion of cousins, first, second, or third does not exist. The children of one sibling called all their mother's sisters their mothers, and the sisters called their siblings' children, their children. Nana must have done a great job, because we children did not miss our biological mother. My older siblings especially, because they had known her. I did not know her to begin with, and so I have nothing to compare the two mothers. One thing I am sure of is that I did not miss out on motherly love, given the way Nana treated me and my siblings. We made sure we returned that love. From the way we loved and treated Nana, nobody other than those who knew of her sister's passing would have known that she was not our real mother.

Nana, full name Nana Akuba Nda, was the third of grandmother Badwo's four children with Opanin Nda. Tall, with jet black skin, a broad face and big eyes she had a presence that made everyone feel protected. She and Azira, our biological mother, were the closest among the siblings, and so it felt natural that she would be the one taking care of Azira's children when she died. I am told everyone who saw them thought they were twins, although Nana was five years older than our mother. Azira served as her sister's bridesmaid when Nana married and moved with her husband to the gold mining town of Obuasi, a booming town about two hundred kilometres northeast of Aakonu. She stayed with Nana and her husband for about a month before returning home. Nana gave her lots of gifts. Azira wore some of the jewelry her sister had given her for her own puberty rites a few years later. Till this day, some of the jewelry Nana gave her sister are still part of the family heirloom.

When Azira got married, Nana was at her side as expected. Before long Azira had had four children. Whenever Azira needed help with her children and their mother was not available, Nana was always there. Unfortunately, Nana was not so lucky—she could not have any children. Someone else may have been jealous of her sister. Not Nana. She adored her sister and her children, and stayed genuinely happy for her. When she got the news that Azira had passed away during the birth of her last child, me, Nana was inconsolable. It is said that when her husband protested and asked that she choose between staying married to him and taking care of us, she did not miss a beat.

A contraction arrives. I stifle a scream and make a face.

I wouldn't want to scream loudly and add to their anxiety. It is not that I could fool them, anyway. With fifteen pregnancies between the two of them and even more deliveries, they can easily tell how much pain I am in. It has been over eight hours now since my water broke and Nana, with whom I have been staying since I was seven months pregnant, called Bozoma, the traditional birth attendant, to oversee the delivery. Bozoma sent for her assistant, a younger woman named Enoku when she realized this was going to be an unusual case. The thirty-five-year-old Enoku has been Madam Bozoma's understudy for about five years now. At eighty, the petite, gray-haired Bozoma was advancing in age and needed someone who was more agile to help her. It worked out well since many in Aakonu were beginning to wonder who would be able to do the job as well as Bozoma did when she finally retires. It is said that almost every household in Aakonu has a baby delivered by Bozoma. Many of those babies have gone on to become mothers and grandmothers themselves, and Bozoma has delivered them too.

Going by my previous pregnancies, the baby should have been out by now. I can see the sweat dripping down their worn faces as they try to figure out what is going on with this baby. I try to think of anything that will take my mind off the pain and what could become of me or my baby should anything go wrong.

Not so fast! My mind says.

Nana comes into the enclosure, consults with the two women, and then leaves quickly without looking me in the eye. She is holding in one hand a piece of my waistcloth, which she hides under her cover cloth. She must be on her way to see Priestess Yaba. This looks serious, and I recall my dear friend Ebela. Will I be next?

Ebela of the slender figure was considered the beauty of our time. She was married at fifteen to an elderly man from our village. Oh, how jealous we were of her good fortune! Her husband was a self-made man with a big house in a big compound. He had three other wives, two of whom had children older than Ebela. The girls among these children had also been married. The oldest child lived with her own husband in a compound not far from her father's.

Being married to a man of one's father's age or older is no girl's idea of a future. It wasn't that of Ebela and the rest of us girls of the village. But do we have a choice? Maybe, maybe not.

Ebela was the talk of the town when she and the rest of the girls her age, including myself, were taken through the puberty rites. This is a rite of passage from childhood to adulthood and is performed for the girls shortly after their first menstrual period. For most girls the first day of menstruation is the first they ever know that such a thing will happen to them. Sexuality and sex education are taboo subjects in the community. My older sister Mua told me how one morning she woke up to find herself on a wet bed. She was sleeping on a raffia mat on the floor of our mother's hut with our two brothers Angama and Nda, myself, and Manu, my mother's second daughter. At first Mua thought she had wet herself. She was too ashamed to get out of bed, fearing that the rest of us would notice. Raffia mats do not absorb liquid. It either stays on the bed or goes straight under. Anyone lying nearby is likely to get wet also. Mua could count the number of times she had woken from sleep because one of us had peed on the mat and had made all of us wet.

Mua waited, pretending to be fast asleep, until the rest of us had woken up and made our way to the compound to start our chores. She fretted. She, the eldest girl, had wet the bed! Meanwhile, Nana was screaming her name, calling her to wake up and join the other girls to go to the river to draw water. Startled by Nana's bellowing, Mua jumped out of bed, covering her wet clothes with her hands. She looked down at her hands and realized that the wetness was due not to water but blood. She started to sob. Nana could not help but come into the room and hold her.

"What is happening to me? Am I going to die? Have I caught a disease?" Mua asked.

Had she wronged someone or done anything to cause them to

"give her" to one of the gods. Being "given to the gods" is actually something to be alarmed about. The gods impose a very stringent code of conduct on our village. They seem to be always waiting around for someone to bring a complaint about what Kwame or Ama has done. But they don't always need anyone to tell them. They know what people are doing all the time. A wrong move, a quarrel, even an unintended argument can bring one to the gods' attention, resulting in sickness, an accident, or even death to that person or even someone from their extended family.

"I am so sorry, Maame, but I haven't done anything wrong," Mua cried.

Nana looked at her scared face and said calmly, "Mua, you are not going to die. Don't be afraid. This is normal. It is not a punishment from the gods. It shows you that you are now a woman. I have been wondering when this was going to happen."

I don't need a soothsayer to tell me where Nana is going now. In her mind there is a reason for my prolonged labour, which we, mere mortals, are not be able to understand. She takes two white eggs and two brown eggs together with a pot of white clay and my waist cloth and heads off to Priestess Yaba's compound.

Ahu, Ebela: Coming of Age

DON'T GET ME WRONG. IT HASN'T been all bad. I have fond memories of growing up in Aakonu. We lived carefree lives as kids. We did our daily chores like sweeping the compound, drawing water from the community well (or the river during the rainy season when the river was less salty), ran errands for the adults if they needed, and spent much time between the river and the sea. We learned to swim, collect shellfish from the river, chase, trap, and catch crabs from the sandy beach, and followed fishermen to pick up some of their catch. Every adult was like a mother or father to us. If they found us doing anything wrong, they had every right to rebuke and sometimes even to cane us. Our existence gave the true meaning to the saying "It takes a village to raise a child."

It feels like yesterday when Ebela and I went through our puberty rites. It was a Thursday. While some families made a big deal of these rites, my family couldn't because we had limited means. The elders were able to scrape together only the basic items that were required—a sizable rooster and a hen donated by one of my mother's sisters, some fresh fish donated by one of my grandmother's relatives, and some smoked fish from an earlier catch. These were used to make large pots of palm-nut soup, peanut butter soup, and light soup. Rice, ampesi, and fufu were cooked to go with the soups. Another relative provided a gourd of fresh palm wine to top off the meal. The night before, I had been smeared with a concoction of shea butter and other ingredients to help tone my body and make me look fresh and fully moisturized. I felt as though the entire process had been undertaken to turn me from an ugly duckling into a graceful swan for the big display. In the morning I sat on a small stool in the yard, smeared with even more of the shea butter concoction. I wore the most colourful beads I had ever seen around my waist, with a wrapper covering a part of it. Nana put her best precious beads around my neck as well. Other girls, friends, and people from the village came around and helped to cook the food on open fires in the compound. It was a happy occasion. Since many of my friends were also friends of Ebela, after helping out at my place they proceeded to Ebela's. Some went to Ebela's first and then came to mine. There was a lot of talking; some people teased me about possible suitors, and how there would soon be a lot of catcalls around our compound. Some of the more daring boys came around, cracked jokes with the women and girls, and then darted off.

The soups took long to cook. While one group took care of the soups, another group pounded the fufu, a third one cooked the rice and ampesi. Fufu is a favourite staple in my village. It is made from boiling cassava and plantain, and then pounding them together into something similar to mashed potato. It is eaten with any soup. To Nana and the elderly people in our village, food meant fufu. I remember how on numerous occasions, when someone asked Nana if she had eaten yet, she would say she had not eaten for days. She meant she had not eaten fufu. If Nana ate a big dinner of assorted foods, she would still say she went to bed hungry, so long as she had not eaten fufu. Give her a good bowl of fufu with her favourite soup, and you would make her day.

Finally the food was ready. My friends and I ate together from a big bowl—a kind of VIP bowl. Everyone wanted to be part of my group. It was my day, and I was the centre of attention. Food was dished out in bowls for people grouped by age. Soon everyone was full from the food and drinks. Then came the time to wash, down at the river. We talked, giggled, and laughed as we made our way to the riverside, recalling how not long ago we had been kids running around naked, how we fought over our wooden dolls and toys and, later, boys. Where had the time gone? Too bad our happy-go-lucky days would soon be over. After puberty rites came marriage, then motherhood. Did we want to spoil the mood today by thinking about all that? No. We had better enjoy ourselves and make the most of the day before it too flew away. Nana had put my clothes in a colourful steel suitcase known, for some reason, as "airtight." One of the girls carried it ahead of us to the riverside. Soon we were joined by Ebela and her entourage. We played many games at the river bank. Everyone, even the young ones knew how to swim. The river was just a playground for us. Finally Ebela and I were given a ceremonial wash in the river. You would think everything associated with our childhood was being cleaned out of our system. When we were finally brought out of the river, our minders (older girls who had already gone through the rites) dressed us up in beautiful clothes. Ebela's dress was a three-piece kente, a very expensive hand-woven cloth associated with royalty, and she was adorned with beautiful golden necklaces, a matching pair of gold earrings, and bracelets. I was dressed in a two-piece high-end cotton cloth (asohyen[1]) and accessorized with a beautiful

---

1   This is top end real Dutch wax made by Vlisco. It is bought in six yard bundles and custom sewn in various styles

piece of kente, beautiful golden necklaces, a matching pair of gold earrings, and bracelets. This particular pair was one of three that Nana had given to my mother, Azira, when she accompanied her to Obuasi as her bridesmaid. Obuasi's reputation as a major gold producing town in the country meant there were also a lot of very skilled goldsmiths. It is said that they could make anything a customer could dream up, so long as it is made of gold. To signify her wish of fertility for her sister, Nana had given Azira a matching pair of necklace, earrings and bracelets, with the design of an *Akuaba* doll, the symbol of fertility, which I wore on my special day. Ebela and I both wore elegant locally made sandals called ahenema. Our heads were adorned with beautiful headgear (duku). We were unrecognizable. It was as if we had become new women within just three weeks, and today was the "homecoming." This was our day, one of the few such days in our lives as young girls, and now young women, when we were the centre of attention.

The first few days afterwards are a blur. I saw a sudden change in Nana's treatment of me. Now I was supposed to know what was expected of me. I was a "woman" and had to be on my best behaviour, make sure that Nana's compound was clean all the time. You never know when a suitor would come over, and a dirty compound would not be a good way to present oneself to a prospective husband.

I remember the day the Tankase (from "Town Council") officers came to Aakonu, having been dispatched from the district office in Axim. I was about eight years old at the time. It was their practice to go round the various villages and towns in the district in groups of four, arresting and giving huge fines to those people who were not maintaining good hygiene in and around their compounds. Those who could not pay the fines could end up doing back-breaking communal labour. Sometimes an entire village could be "arrested" by these feared men. If they found a culprit too poor to pay the fine or too old to do communal labour, they would make the person stand in the sun, hold his ears, and jump up and down singing,

"*Menzo yese mende edwεkε, Menzo yεsε mende edwεkε,*"
meaning,
"*I am stubborn, I don't listen, I am stubborn, I don't listen,*"
until their worn limbs failed to move any more.

It was around seven thirty in the morning. Usually someone gave the alarm when they were spotted coming from the river's edge. Not that day. There was no alarm. It turned out that one of them knew how to paddle the canoe and so they were able to ferry themselves effortlessly to our end of the river and make their way to Aakonu unnoticed. The sun was already rising, but we had yet to sweep the compound. Unwashed bowls from the previous night's dinner sat on the floor in the kitchen, where there were also scattered the ashes from the firewood in the *mokyea* used for cooking. On top of the walls behind the kitchen and in the compound were scattered droppings from chicken and sheep.

There was no way we could clean all this before the dreadful Tankase arrived at our compound. Nana decided to take Mua, Manu, my brothers, and me to hide in the think mangrove a few metres behind our street. For the next three hours we hid watching the furious Tankase turn our kitchen and compound upside down. The entire village looked deserted. We watched as Opanin Kabenla, a tall, elderly man of about seventy-five, who could not run and hide, was made to do the jump until he collapsed into the sand in front of the officers. We stayed in our hideout until we got the signal that they were finally gone. When we were back in our compound, Nana vowed to ensure that we wake up by five-thirty in the morning and do our chores before anything else. Mua and Manu's job was to sweep the kitchen and fill the water containers, my brothers swept the compound and cleaned the hen coop, and I refreshed the mokyea and washed the dishes.

Now that Mua and Manu had married and left for their own homes, the job of keeping Nana's compound clean, the water containers filled, and the dishes washed fell on me.

I had to perfect my cooking skills as well. I had heard more than once the story of a girl who got married and moved with her husband to a faraway land. But she had never learned the art of cooking well. Her mother, rather than teach her, made excuses for her. This everybody knew and so nobody came to ask for her hand in marriage. Finally a stranger who had no knowledge of her deficiency married her and went away with her, but he soon realized that she could not cook. One day, when after a long day on the farm he came home, his wife served him hot water with boiled palm nuts, calling it palm nut soup. He could not tolerate this and sent her home with the so-called soup. She could not stand the humiliation and ran away into the forest, never to be seen again.

In no way would I, Mame Ahu, allow myself to suffer the same fate. Have I done well in the cooking department? Well, let's just say that I haven't been sent home because of my soup, so I must have done well.

When, three months after our puberty rites, I heard that a suitor had come to ask for my friend Ebela's hand in marriage, I was torn. On one hand I was happy for her. It was the expected next step after the rites. With Ebela's good looks and her better family fortune it was a no brainer that she would find a suitor soon. Was

I jealous? Yes, I was.

Everyone in the village wanted to know who the man was. I had no doubt it would be the dashing young man Mozu. He was about nineteen years old, tall, well built with a strong chest and already on track to taking after his father. From a very early age, Mozu had worked on his father's canoe. His father owned one of the three fishing canoes in Aakonu. The people of Aakonu were mostly fishermen. This meant that the three canoe-owners employed most of the able-bodied men of the village. The few who did not work as fishermen were small-scale farmers. One can imagine how much power and influence the canoe-owners wielded. To me, nothing would have been more romantic than for beautiful Ebela to settle down with dashing Mozu. A young couple charting their course in life together. The thought made me smile. I began daydreaming about the other boys my friends and I had been singing about during our Anyima gatherings.

Anyima! Now that is one game that brings a smile to the face of many Nzema girls. Usually girls of ages thirteen and over played it. It was when all the secret crushes came out. At around seven PM, girls finished their chores and made a dash for the village square. Any group of three or more could play Anyima, but it was better enjoyed with more people. Since many girls were married off by age seventeen, the girls who came to play Anyima were usually between eleven and seventeen. Older women also played, but only on special occasions, like when someone died who had loved the game. In such instances friends of the deceased would come together and play it as a way of remembering her. A group of about ten girls formed a big circle. One girl moved to the centre and started an Anyima song. As she sang, the rest of the girls clapped their hands in unison while singing the chorus. When she finished, she joined the circle and the next girl in line replaced her. They did this until everyone had sung. The person in the centre of the circle could choose to change the song. The singer would mention the name of her crush or boyfriend. The other girls might not be aware of this. This was where the excitement came, as people got to confirm their suspicions about the girls' crushes. I remember clearly one night when we were playing and it got to Ebela's turn, she went into the centre of the circle and started singing:

Ayi ma menga mengilɛ wɔ
Ayi ma menga mengilɛ wɔ
Meka mahile wɔ kɛ
Me yeye nu mahile wɔ kɛ
Ele kpale a ɛnrɛdo me hu Mozu o yieeee

The rest of us joined in:

Chorus
Ayi o, ma menga mengilɛ wo o daa
Ele kpale a ɛnrɛdo me hu Mozu o yieeee

Translation:
Friend let me tell you
Friend let me tell you
I tell you that
I tell you without a doubt
That no matter how good you are,
You will never match my husband Mozu o yeaah

Chorus
Friend let me tell you now and again
That no matter how good you are,
You will never match my husband Mozu o yeaah

Ebela's mention of Mozu all of a sudden brought up a great deal of excitement. Many of us had already suspected that Ebela and Mozu might be on to something. Now that she had

mentioned his name, it confirmed our suspicion that there had
to be something going on between them, and the anticipation
rose among us that after the puberty rites he would be the one
asking for her hand in marriage. Perhaps many of us saw such a
match as a confirmation of our own expectations for ourselves.
The ability to marry someone we loved and could relate to, even
play with, rather than the usual custom of being married off to a
man old enough to be our fathers, who had co-wives of the same
age or even older than our mothers. It is said that many young
women had had a hard time transitioning from seeing someone as
a father to suddenly becoming their wives. There was a story told
of a young wife who kept calling her husband "Father" and her
co-wife "Mother," until the older wife told her that if she was her
daughter they wouldn't be sharing the same man.

There was much disappointment then when it turned out that
Ebela's suitor was not Mozu. If the young man had any such
thoughts, having to compete with Egya Amakyi, the prominent
elder in the village, was a battle he was sure to lose.

Aso: Mother of Angels

THE STORY OF ASO, Egya Amakyi's first wife, is difficult to recount. For anyone to be faced with such misfortune in the midst of plenty is something that beats the mind. She married Amakyi when he was a young man and stood by his side as his wealth increased. A hard-working woman, she tilled the land he inherited from his father. It was said that the coconuts she planted on that farm were what brought the money that Amakyi used to buy his first fishing net. As his wealth increased, Aso's fortunes dwindled. Her first son, a handsome baby boy, died within two weeks following his birth. She had been healthy throughout the pregnancy—it is rumoured that the day she went into labour, she had carried a basinful of fresh fish to Kamunu to sell.

While the men fished, it was the job of the women to sell the fish. Every day after the men brought in the catch, they would sort out the bigger ones from the small ones. The women were then invited to come and negotiate their prices. There was no weighing scale; instead, a bowl with the capacity to hold about two and a half pounds of fish was used. The smaller fish were priced by the bowl. Some thirty minutes were spent negotiating the price of a bowlful. The agreed price depended on the quantity of supply, the season, and the time of day. The catch that came in early morning to mid-afternoon commanded a higher price because there were more customers then.

The bigger fish were sold individually by their type and size. The buyers' representative normally just took a look at a fish, sometimes picked it up to gauge its weight, and then quoted her price. Then bargaining began.

Some women preferred to smoke the fish in a clay oven until they were well dried, before taking them to Ayinam, NewTown, and other bigger towns nearby to sell on market days. Others ran with their fresh fish straight to Kamunu and Bokabo, which were five and ten kilometres away respectively. These inland communities relied on sellers like Aso from Aakonu and other coastal villages for their fish.

Aso was a regular at the seashore and was known by the other women as a top negotiator and a very good saleswoman. So while the role of negotiator was not assigned to any specific person, when Aso was around she usually ended up negotiating.

This particular day started just like any other. Although heavily pregnant, she went to the shore with her big basin and tray as usual. She led the price negotiations, which resulted in what they all considered a great deal. She purchased sixty pounds of the small fish and forty of the larger ones, for a total cost of two hundred shillings. She carried her load straight to the dock to catch the canoe to take her to the other side, where she continued her journey to Kamunu on foot. She had been feeling lower abdominal pains since morning but didn't think much of it. Fortunately, the canoe was on her side of the river when she arrived. She put her load into it, rowed to the other end, carried her load and walked briskly along the five-kilometre footpath to Kamunu. She felt a wetness as soon as she arrived and started to put down her load. With this first pregnancy, she didn't know what to expect when she went into labour. She naively thought that she had soiled herself.

Aso left her fish in the care of a friendly customer and asked to excuse herself. She went behind the kitchen of one of the compounds close to the market to check herself. That was when she saw what she was later told was the "show," a thick mucus covering the cervix that comes out at the onset of labour. Within minutes, her waters broke and she could hardly walk. She gave out a loud cry, drawing the attention of the women in the compound. Knowing that she was heavily pregnant, they rushed to her help. They took her to a makeshift bathroom in the compound, and soon realized that the baby was already on the way. One of them put her cover cloth on the clay floor and helped Aso onto it. Word spread around that Aso was in labour.

Aso was in unbearable pain. Her screams could be heard into the distance, calling out Amakyi's name and vowing never to go through this again.

"Noo, this is too painful. Amakyi, why would you do this to me? I do not want to see your face ever again."

That, to many people, is the irony of childbirth. At the height of the pain most women swear never to go through it again. Delivery room nurses know all about this. They hear women say all sorts of things against their husbands. Once the baby is born, however, most women forget they ever said any such thing. Most take one look at their babies and fall in love forever. They would never change a thing. Others do struggle with postpartum depression. But what the mothers need is support that is nonjudgemental.

Till today many in that compound smile when this episode

about Aso's delivery is brought up. Soon, with a few more pushes Aso delivered a bouncy baby boy to everyone's relief. One of the two women who were attending her cut the umbilical cord, cleaned and wrapped the screaming baby in another cover cloth, while the other one helped her deliver the placenta. Soon mother and baby were resting comfortably in the living room. It was then that it dawned on Aso how fortunate she had been. A lot could have gone wrong. Here she was in a village away from her own. What if there had been complications? What if there hadn't been enough experienced people around? She was lucky it was a Friday, when many in this Muslim community stayed at home. If it had been any other day most of the women would have gone to their farms. She would not have been so fortunate.

The women made her hot pepper soup, which Aso finished in no time. One of her friends, Ebakyi, had also come to sell her fish. When she saw a stranger taking care of Aso's fish, she asked where Aso was. When she heard that Aso was in labour, she left to inform the husband and family.

Amakyi and Aso's family did not wait. As soon as they heard the message they rushed to Kamunu to see the mother and child. Amakyi was over the moon. He could not believe his good fortune. The birth of a son is a sign of good luck, an assurance that the family name will continue. He chided Aso for not listening when he told her to stop trading at that late stage in her pregnancy. What he had feared most almost happened. What if she had gone into labour in the night while they were on their way home from Kamunu? In the absence of any light even the most experienced birth attendant would have difficulty attending to her on the narrow footpath between the two villages. Aso apologized, but who would want to keep imagining the bad that could have happened when celebrating a happy occasion?

Aso needed another day of rest to regain her strength before making the journey back to Aakonu. And so Amakyi and the other family members departed, and Aso's mother stayed with her. The next morning their host woke up early, made hot water for Aso's bath and treatment, and served them a good breakfast. By lunchtime, mother and baby, in the company of Aso's mother and two people from the compound in Kamunu where Aso had delivered her baby, made the trip back to Aakonu. It was a joyous return. Aso enjoyed the remainder of her rest period in the comfort of her husband's compound. Her mother, excited about another grandson in the family, had already moved in to take care of her daughter and grandson. This is the norm in the community. In their third trimester of pregnancy most women move back to their mother's home, so that she can help them through any complications. Women who are with their husbands far away from home usually make the journey back home. In situations where the man is well off or has no concerns about the mother-in-law coming to stay in his compound, she comes to stay with them. If she has her hands full with other grandchildren, then her pregnant daughter comes to stay with her.

The next week was uneventful. Every day the new mother was treated to a rich bowl of fufu and palm nut soup with snails, dried fish, and cocoyam leaves. Cocoyam leaves and palm nut soup help the new mother's milk to flow. All Aso had to do was wake up, go through the treatment process of squatting on hot water (steam was believed to help get rid of the bad blood from her system) and take her bath, and then be smeared with shea butter from head to toe. She wore white bead necklaces and bracelets. Various sweet-scented spices were smeared on her upper body. The ten days following the birth would be the best in Aso's entire married life. Baby Kofi (so named because he was born on Friday) latched on to the breast well and was filling out nicely. Aso loved how fresh she herself looked and how rested she felt. She had many helpers with her baby. Apart from her own mother, who dropped everything to come and stay with her, there were also Amakyi's siblings and their wives in the compound. Everyone was fond of their sister-in-law and their new son (actually, nephew).

On Thursday, a day before Kofi turned two weeks, Aso noticed a change in the way he suckled. Initially she thought he was tired. She let him rest, then tried feeding him again in the night but he wouldn't take the breast. She was surprised but didn't think too much of it. But the next morning she began to get worried. She told her mother about this. Her mother checked the baby and thought he could be constipated. She gave him enema and bathed him with warm water. This seemed to help a little. He sucked a little when Aso gave him the breast. He fell asleep and Aso put him on his mat and went to have her bath. When she returned and touched her baby he did not respond. She let out a loud cry. Her mother took the baby from her and having looked at him, screamed for Amakyi. Initially they all thought it was con-vulsion (*anwuma*). They put Kofi at the edge of the thatched roof and poured water on the roof. The water falling off the roof was believed to heal convulsions. Unfortunately this did not work. Amakyi took his son from his mother-in-law and ran to Priestess Yaba's compound.

The compound housed several huts. It had two sections. In the outer section was the kitchen, a gazebo-like hut where reg-ular visitors sat and a bigger hut where "in-patients" who were receiving treatment at the shrine lived. In the inner section, with its own gate, were the Priestess's hut, the shrine, and a wide open area where worship services took place every Tuesday and Friday. Inside the inner section, Amakyi put baby Kofi down at the foot of the shrine, the symbol of Priestess Yaba's power. The shrine, which sat under a special shed beside Priestess Yaba's hut, consisted of a raised cement block covered with a rectangular piece of red calico, on which stood a large circular wooden bowl. In the bowl sat six medium-sized wooden figurines, each representing one of the gods that she spoke for. The figurines were arranged in a circle around a small white basin filled with water and Florida water perfume. A small canopy was put over the wooden bowl, on which was hung about two yards of white calico. In front of the wooden bowl an opening had been made in the cement block in which two scented candles burned. Two specially marked divination cups stood beside the wooden bowl. The lavender from the scented candles and the Florida water gave the area around the shrine a warm, relaxing feel.

As she did every Friday morning before the main worship service in the afternoon, Priestess Yaba, a middle-aged woman, sat beside her shrine, on a specially carved wooden stool known locally as Sesegua. She used this time to commune with the gods and to provide divination to those who needed to consult with them. The circular markings of white clay on the outer joints of her arms and legs, and two markings across her eyes were especially visible against her chocolate-coloured skin. She wore a white calico wrapper round her waist. Another piece of white calico, which she used as a cover cloth, was wrapped around her midsection in place of a blouse and hung loosely over her shoulder. Her thick, coiled hair was braided in two parts, each part held together by six cowries on a string. In her hand she held a white fly whisk (*bodua*), which she turned around from time to time, as if in response to a beat only she could hear. She looked like she was just waking up from a trance.

It was believed that Priestess Yaba was in constant contact with her gods. Even when she was doing mundane things like eating, one could not help but think that she was possessed.

Amakyi knelt in front of her, one open hand in the other like a child expecting a gift from a powerful elder. Aso and her mother, who had followed Amakyi but had not been able to catch up with him, soon arrived and prostrated before the priestess, beside him.

For a while the Priestess seemed to be engrossed in something other than the distraught man who knelt before her. It turned out that one of her gods had already told her a sick child was being brought to her. She was busy negotiating in the spirit for the boy's healing, hence her inability to respond to Amakyi and his wife and mother-in-law. After what seemed like eternity to them, Priestess Yaba motioned to them to get up and take a seat. She took the child in her arms and began to shake as she went into another trance. She looked at Amakyi, then Aso, and then her mother. When she spoke, it sounded like gibberish. Seeing how lost they seemed, Adwo, one of the Priestess's apprentices, a young girl about fifteen years old, came over to stand by them so she could interpret the Priestess's actions and sounds to them.

The Priestess got up from her *Sesegua* and began to dance with the baby in her arms, talking to herself. This was nothing new to Amakyi and his people. Fetish priests and priestesses were the go-to people for ailments. They were the interpreters of the gods. People believed that every affliction they suffered was a punishment by the gods for a wrong they had done someone, who had complained to them. If you went to the gods early enough and did as you were told, you could avert the punishment. Whether or not the gods chose to heal was their prerogative. The priestess stopped her dancing and started pacing; finally she said she had a message from the gods. She looked at Aso and asked:

"Aso, have you offended anyone?"

Aso had no idea what she meant. She was too distraught even to think straight. Her mother answered for her.

"My Priestess, she would not know what to say. Like the elders say, she who is making a road would not know that it is crooked. In her current state, Aso is not able to tell if she has done anything that someone would consider offensive. Could the gods give her some clue?"

The Priestess paced about again. This time in slow, deliberate steps. As she did so she flipped the fly whisk, which she still held in one hand, the other hand wrapped around baby Kofi. She touched his joints with the tip of the fly whisk. After a while, she placed Kofi where Amakyi had laid him and sat down on her Sesegua.

Priestess Yaba motioned to Adwo to fetch her divination cup. Adwo picked one of the cups from the shrine, topped up the water in it, then she knelt before the Priestess and handed it to her. The Priestess took the cup, looked intently into it for about three minutes, reciting some incantations under her breath. She stopped abruptly, turned to Aso and asked her, "Have you cultivated a piece of land along the footpath to Bokabo?"

Aso answered, "Yes. That land belongs to my husband, and he cleared it for me to use for our cassava and coconut plantations."

The priestess nodded and went on, "Do you remember that when your husband went to burn the cleared area, the fire also burnt a portion of the neighbouring farm?"

"Yes," Amakyi answered this time. He remembered the episode well. It was a Thursday afternoon. He had cleared his land two weeks earlier and was waiting for it to dry before burning it. Instead, it had rained the first three days. The next few days there was sunshine and so when he heard it was going to be raining again over the weekend, he decided to do the burning that day, although people were not supposed to be at the farm on Thursdays. Mother Earth, known as Azɛlɛ Yaba, is said to have been born on a Thursday, therefore nobody from Aakonu was expected to do any major work on the farm on Thursdays. As if to punish Amakyi for breaking this unwritten rule, the fire he set soon spread beyond his farm, burning a sizable chunk of his neighbour Minla's farm. But for the presence of a stream close by, the fire would have devastated an even larger area. Amakyi himself was lucky to have escaped unhurt. He was so shaken he could not leave his house for days.

When Minla visited his farm the next day and saw what had happened to it, he was furious. He suspected that Amakyi intentionally did what he did because he coveted his farm. It was later, when Amakyi went to Minla's house and explained what had happened that he changed his mind.

"My Priestess, it did and I spoke about it to Minla, who owns that land. He did not seem worried," Amakyi said.

"Well," the priestess responded. "He was not happy about it. He complained while coming home from his farm that you had not respected his property, and that this was your attempt to steal his land, because he did not have the money or the resources to cultivate it. One of the gods who guards the land around the farm heard his complaint and has decided to punish you by taking something that is very precious to you, your son."

This hit Amakyi and Aso like a thunderbolt. These gods were always inserting themselves into people's lives. They had made themselves police and judges. They lurked around every hill, bush, well, stream, and river. Someone you might have offended could go to such a god or spirit with an egg and implore them to harm you. In the case of Amakyi and Aso, Minla had questioned the real motive behind Amakyi's actions and wondered out aloud if it wasn't a ploy to relieve him of his land. He had not intentionally "given" Amakyi to that god.

"What can we do about this, My Priestess?" Amakyi asked.

Priestess Yaba continued with her divination for a while, before looking up from her cup. She spoke slowly in a soft voice, as if the words she was speaking were being dictated to her: "The god wants a sacrifice of one red cock and one white hen and six eggs, half a bottle of palm oil, a yard of white calico, a block of white clay, a bottle of gin, and a basin full of palm wine. You must produce these before sunrise tomorrow morning. We will have to take these items to the farm, and conduct the sacrifice before the day ends tomorrow. We will know by then whether the sacrifice has been accepted or not. Only then will we know little Kofi's fate."

Aso was inconsolable. Why her? Why them? Why their little Kofi? She would do anything for her beautiful baby boy. How could the gods be so callous? Amakyi asked permission to go and find the items that had been requested by the priestess. Fortunately, money was no problem. Even if he did not have it, Amakyi would have done whatever it took to save his son. There was nothing he would not get.

Some people were usually not as lucky. There was a family who were given a list of things to bring for a sacrifice to save their daughter, who was suffering from an abscess on the breast. Based on the description that the family provided, she might have had breast cancer. Unfortunately the villagers did not know better. They spent all their energy trying to find the items requested for the sacrifice. The young lady died before they could get them, and the family had to contend with the thought that their inability to get the required items had caused her death.

In baby Kofi's case, the priestess advised them that leaving her yard before the sacrifice was completed would expose the baby to the anger of the god who, at that point, was holding Kofi's soul hostage. She suggested that Aso and her mother stay in her compound with the baby. Meanwhile, baby Kofi continued to be lethargic and wouldn't suckle. Aso put up a brave face, encouraged that the requested items would be procured soon enough and her son would recover once the sacrifice was made. Amakyi was able to get the items and was at the priestess's yard before sunrise the next day. As soon as she received the items, Priestess Yaba, Adwo her apprentice, one of her drummers named Noba, a young man whose life Priestess Yaba is said to have saved from imminent death, and who had since devoted himself to her service, Amakyi and Aso's mother took off for the farm. Adwo carried the items in a basin, covered with a piece of white calico. When they got to the river's edge, the canoe was on the other side.

Noba did not waste time. He stripped to his underpants and swam to the end to fetch the canoe so they could continue on their important assignment. Ironically, three people who were coming from Bokabo got to the dock just when he reached that side of the river. He got into the canoe, helped the three people into it, and paddled across to where the Priestess and the rest of them were waiting. Noba carried the Priestess on his back and helped her get into the canoe. As she was on a mission for another god, it was not good for her to step in the Amanzule River due to the latter's jealousy. Once they got across, Noba carried her on his back as they waded through the small stream that lay between the dock and the shoreline. Soon they were on their way to the farm to perform the sacrifice.

Based on the advice of Priestess Yaba, Aso remained in the yard with her son. She lay beside him on a mat under the shed where the shrine was, scared that being anywhere else would expose him to danger. She watched over him like a hawk, very hopeful that he would get well soon, now that the sacrifice was being offered.

But when she checked after a while, she saw that Kofi had stopped breathing. She screamed. "Somebody help me!" she cried. "My baby, my baby . . . " People ran in from the adjacent compound to see what was going on. Initially they hesitated when they saw that Aso was crying from the shrine. A woman in her forties whose hut was just outside the compound, named Manza, rushed to the shed, picked Kofi up, put him on her back and used her extra cover cloth to hold him in place. She ran as fast as her legs could carry her. She got to the riverside just as the canoe was being tethered. Aso could not keep up with her. She was so distraught she felt glued to the spot. The young man who was tethering the canoe offered to paddle it for Manza so that she did not need to.

Once she got down on the other side, Manza continued her brisk walk to the farm. She got there just as Priestess Yaba was starting to offer the sacrifice. Everyone froze when they saw Manza with Kofi. Manza was breathless from her brisk walk. Amakyi took his son from her back. He was lifeless. Amakyi gave Kofi to the priestess. Ashen-faced, the priestess shook her head as she held his lifeless little body in her hands. She put the boy on her chest and ran into the bush. Amakyi tried to follow her but he was held back by Noba. According to him, the Priestess was going to confront the god, and so it would not be good for Amakyi to tag along. He could not see a god even if it stood in front of him, and this was a mission for only those who could see in the spirit. It was thirty minutes later when Priestess Yaba emerged from the bush. This must be one stubborn god. He had decided he could not wait for the sacrifice and took Kofi's soul before they could start. Manza wrapped the baby and helped Aso's mother carry her grandson's lifeless body home. Aso was waiting for them by the river on the other side.

The grief-stricken couple brought Kofi home and prepared him for burial.

Aso changed from that day onwards. She could not mourn her baby because of the belief in Aakonu that a mother should not mourn the death of a first child, for fear of not being able to have any more children. She showed a brave face externally, but in her heart she mourned and cried over what her son could have been. Seeing anyone with a child her son's age was especially difficult.

It was a great relief when she became pregnant a second time. Unfortunately, her second child, a daughter, could not live beyond her third month. This time the cause, according to the priestess, was the result of an argument Aso had had with one of her husband's sisters. Aso was distraught. When she had her third child, a boy, they decided to give him the name "Fovole," or Garbage.

People believed that if they gave a disgusting name to a child, a child-stealing spirit would be put off. It seemed to have worked, for Fovole seemed to thrive for a while, until his second birthday when there was a major measles outbreak in Aakonu. People remember that outbreak to this day. It happened just after the enstoolment of the new Chief, Nana Ngoma II. There had been a lot of celebration and so parents were too busy to pay attention to the small rashes that seemed to appear so suddenly all over the body of their children. When Aso realized that her son's temperature was so high and he wouldn't eat anything, she and Amakyi rushed him once again to the Priestess's compound. There were about twelve other children in the same situation, ranging in age from three months to five years. Priestess Yaba was already in action, dressed in her usual white calico wrapper and another piece of white calico cloth covering her top and tied at her back. She held in her hand the white bodua which she used to touch the sick children as they lay in their mothers' arms. She kept flipping the bodua around while she did so. All this while her mouth moved as if she was talking, but no words came out. When she got to Fovole, she stopped abruptly and called out forcefully to Noba, her drummer, to start playing the drum, emphasizing with her hands how intensely she wanted it played. Amakyi and Aso listened intently, wondering why the Priestess seemed so animated once she touched their child with her *bodua*. As Noba played the drum, the Priestess, now very animated, started singing, imploring her gods to act. The people joined in the singing. They were clapping as well. It was a very animated crowd. Priestess Yaba danced to the beat of the drum. At one point she twisted herself so much everyone was sure it was the snake god that had possessed her. Each of her six gods represented by the six wooden figures manifests differently. It is said that the nature of the manifestation indicates the nature of that god. For instance, there is the young woman god who likes to flirt with the drummer and any man around when she possesses Priestess Yaba. There is the drunkard who makes her walk like she was intoxicated. It is said that the drunkard lives in the marshes where the raffia plants grow, and so he always has a lot of *doka* (the drink from the raffia plant) to drink. There is a fierce one who seems more than ready to engage everyone in combat. The other two usually possessed her together, and are said to be a married couple. They keep onlookers mesmerized as they take turns to talk, and love to argue when they possess her. Watching Priestess Yaba talk in a man's voice and then turn around to speak in a woman's voice would win over the strongest skeptic.

It is known among the people of Aakonu that the snake doesn't normally show up unless the issue at stake is very serious. At this point Amakyi and his wife are visibly scared. They kneel before her. She twists and twists, then turns around, stops as abruptly as she had begun, walks quietly to her sesegua and sits down. The drumming and singing stops as if on cue. Adwo, who had been singing with the people goes to stand by her mistress. Priestess Yaba whispers something to her. She comes to Aso and Amakyi and beckons them to get closer to the Priestess. She speaks to them in a very hushed tone, almost like a hiss.

"Aso, Amakyi, your son's situation is very serious. I have tried to wrestle him from River Amanzule. We are still wrestling as I speak to you."

"My Priestess," Amakyi intervened when she was done. "What can we do now?"

"Amakyi, I know you have a good heart, and you are always eager and ready to do whatever the gods ask of you." She paused, as if to recollect her thoughts.

"My son, it is different this time. It is not you alone. As you can see, the same affliction is affecting all the children who have been brought here. The river god is angry. He is asking why this entire village decided to offer him a smaller sheep for this year's sacrifice with the excuse that the various fishing nets had not done too well, only for them to turn around and slaughter three big sheep for Chief Ngoma II's enstoolment. He is very angry, and hence has decided to use the children as his sacrifice."

"My Priestess, you are not going to allow that, are you? Surely you and the gods will intercede for us," Amakyi implored her. Aso opened her mouth but no words came out.

"I will do what I can. River Amanzule is a great friend, but he is also a formidable adversary. You should know by now."

When she was done she signalled for them to get up. She gave

Aso a small bottle filled with the Florida perfumed water from inside the shrine and sent them home. She did the same for the rest of the parents before dispersing them. She asked the parents to put the perfume in their children's bathwater and also use it to spray them whenever their skin became too hot. She was going to retire to her hut early as she had to continue wrestling River Amanzule for the souls of those children.

Seven days later, all but two of the children had died, including Fovole.

To make matters worse for Aso, pressure began to mount on Amakyi to marry another woman since it seemed that his first wife was not able to give him a living child. Aso had seen this coming, but somehow she had convinced herself that her Amakyi would stand by her and they would seek a solution together. They could find a more reliable priestess. They could travel to other places to find a solution. Maybe they could even visit the city, to see what could be done. But Amakyi was already tired of the situation and was more than eager to find himself a second wife. When Aso realized she could not convince her husband not to take a new wife, she decided to help him select one. If she was going to have a rival, she might as well take part in the selection so that she would have some leverage when the new wife came to live with them.

Aso asked around and found a young woman of marriageable age from Kema's compound, just past the community well, on the same street where she and her husband Amakyi lived. Kema and Aso were from the same clan. In fact, both he and Aso were brought up by the same matriarch, Nana Mozuma, who the young woman was named after.

When the young Mozuma agreed to marry Amakyi, Aso was very happy.

She helped Amakyi select the items needed for the knocking and for the marriage itself.

She wanted nothing more than to treat her as a younger sister who would give her husband what she could not give him— healthy, living children. Contrary to what she had thought, the arrival of the young woman in the Amakyi household confirmed Aso's worst fears. Mozuma knew the edge she had over Aso. She was arrogant. She made it clear that Aso was bad luck, and picked quarrels with her at every opportunity. Fortunately for Amakyi and unfortunately for Aso, Mozuma had three children within four years. The two boys and a girl became the centre of Amakyi's life, and with it his love for Aso diminished. Aso, finding herself alone and mindful of what a thin line she had to tread between feeling sorry for herself and being happy for her husband and her rival, decided to lose herself in her work. She tilled the land and undertook the processing of oil from their coconut plantation. While her industry made her household rich, her childlessness made her a pariah in the village. Any time any of Mozuma's children fell sick, Aso worried that the Priestess would blame it on her.

Soon her husband was looking to marry again. This time she really was not happy about it. Now that his second wife Mozuma had given him five children, there was no justification for him to marry again. Aso concluded that Amakyi wanted to marry a third woman just because he could. There was nothing she could say that would change his mind.

Amakyi married Ebela, the young beauty of the village, who had just gone through her puberty rites to be his fourth wife.

By now Aso has reached menopause and has accepted that she will never have a child of her own. As the older and wealthier wife, she tries her best to support the children of her rivals, sponsoring their marriages and being the beloved grandma to their children.

Ebela is young enough to be her daughter, but one thing she has been good at after all these years is to hide her true feelings and her hurt. She now wonders if she should continue to hide her feelings and welcome Ebela wholeheartedly as the new wife, thus setting the right example for her co-wives, or continue to protest until Amakyi changes his mind.

Nana Ngoma II

THE ENSTOOLMENT OF NANA NGOMA II was a truly joyous occasion. The people of Aakonu had cause to rejoice; they had waited two years for this event. The queen mother, Obahemaa Ekeleba, was advancing in age and once she confirmed Somiah, the first son of Kua, the last of her grandmother's three daughters as the one who would occupy the stool, everyone began looking forward to his enstoolment. The critical role of the Obahemaa is to select the rightful successor to the stool. While both she and the chief are co-rulers, her role as kingmaker puts her in an influential position. But she is not the wife of the chief. In Aakonu, the Obahemaa has her own stool next to the chief. She is selected along the same matrilineal line as the chief, and it is she who nominates a new chief when the old chief joins his ancestors. She is recognized as the one who knows the intricate web of matrilineal inheritance and therefore is best suited to identify the next chief. Of the various levels of governance, the chief is the closest to the people. Every community has one. He lives among the people, and is the one they turn to with any issues.

Nana Ngoma II, known in private life as Somiah, was a shy,

unassuming and lanky middle-aged man who did not really want
to be the chief. His uncle, the flamboyant Ngoma I was larger
than life, literally and figuratively. The younger man always felt
intimidated and never saw himself as eventually occupying the
stool when the older one passed. He ran away to Obuasi, the gold
mining town when his uncle fell ill. When he had not returned
to Aakonu after two years, the village people sent a delegation to
Obuasi to bring him home.

Somiah overcame his apprehension and accepted to be chief,
though actually he had no option but to accept. He and the visiting delegation came to an agreement about when he would
return to Aakonu. Two of the members stayed at Obuasi with
him and the rest returned home. The Obahemaa then caused the
gong-gong[2] to be beaten to summon all the people to the palace.
It was around six-thirty PM in the evening. The sun had already
set when the stool messenger, Ngoroma set off with his gong-gong.
He stood in the street beside the communal well and began, hit-
ting a small metal stick against the gong-gong:

"Gong! Gong! Gong! Gong!"

He stopped to make sure he had everyone's attention. People
stopped whatever they were doing and listened. Then he continued in a loud voice:

"Noloooooooo! Yooooooo!

Aakonu Ezoavole Mrɛnya nee Mralɛ

Kɛ Obahemaa nee ye mgbanyinli se yɛzɛ bɛ la ɛne

ɛhyema Molɛ ye, dɔne nwiɔ, yɛhyia bɛ muala wɔ ahenfie

ɛdawɔ mɔɔ wɔama la, ɛto ndane kpole o kpaa yii!!!

Gong! Gong! Gong! Gong!"

"Gong! Gong! Gong! Gong!

Hear Ye! Hear Ye!

---

2   A hollow piece of metal. Used for making announcements before
modern day loudspeakers became popular. Still used in some areas.

Men and women of Aakonu
This is what the queen mother and her elders have asked us to tell you
This Sunday at two pm, we need all of you at the palace.
Anyone who fails to come will face a huge fine kpaa yii!
Gong! Gong! Gong! Gong!"

Ngoroma went on to three more stops on that street to make the announcement. He proceeded to the two other streets and did the same.

That Sunday around three PM the people of Aakonu gathered at the palace. Although the announcement had said two PM, most people as usual saw that as the time to set off from home. When everyone was seated, Obahemaa Ekeleba came out and was helped onto her stool, flanked by the elders. She was nicely dressed in a rich cotton wrapper, a piece of kente worn over her shoulder and a chain of large beads around her neck and on her wrists. Her grey, coiled hair was braided into a puff with a chain of colourful beads.

Her spokesman, Opanin Ekobo, stood up and addressed the gathering.

"Ladies and gentlemen of Aakonu, this is what Nana Obaahema and her elders say to tell you. The delegation from Obuasi has returned with great news. Our new chief will be here by Kundum.[3]"

The exact date of Somiah's arrival was kept a secret. Even then, the idea that they would have a chief by the Kundum festival was enough to get them excited. After three years they would have a Kundum festival in the presence of a chief, and they would spare no effort at making it a memorable one. They let out a loud cheer.

"Agooo! Agooo!" the spokesman sought their attention again.

---

3   A festival celebrated by the people of Aakonu and surrounding areas.

"I know it is exciting news. It also means that there is a lot of work to do. From this week onwards, we all need to ensure that this entire village is as clean as possible. There will be a lot of communal work needed to clear and widen the footpath to the village, to clean, polish, and paint the communal canoe, and to make sure that the palace is in excellent shape."

A committee was set up to plan the upcoming enstoolment and the crowd dispersed. From then on, this was what everyone talked about.

Three weeks after the delegation visited Obuasi, the two elders they had left behind returned with Somiah. They arrived late at night so as not to be noticed. They confined him in a room in the palace for two weeks. This was very important. During this time Somiah would literally transform from a simple, regular man to the wise occupant of the royal stool of Aakonu.

During his confinement he learned the history of the royal family, and about the previous occupants, their strengths and weaknesses, and the lessons learned from their lives that should guide him. He was taken through the different customs and beliefs of the people, the various gods of Aakonu, and what each of them liked, and most importantly what they hated as well. He also needed to understand the customary laws, including the role of the chief within the paramount area. He was bathed in various herbs to fortify him and give him supernatural strength. He had very little contact with people, even his wife could not be with him. His food was specially prepared and tasted in front of him by one of the members of the royal household before he was allowed to eat.

The palace guarded the secret so well that it took a whole week before people began to suspect that their new chief had been confined. All this while beautification work in and around the palace continued.

The enstoolment was set for Friday, two weeks after his confinement, during which he was also expected to pick the name he would like to have once he was enstooled. The young man settled on Ngoma, having been impressed with the wisdom, strength, and magnanimity of his predecessor Ngoma I. Early on the Friday he cast away his confinement clothing and was helped into his royal costume—a pair of gold-coloured shorts and matching short-sleeve shirt of silk, over which was flung a rich and colourful kente. On his finger was a big golden ring, on his neck a long golden chain at the end of which hung a golden elephant, the symbol of the stool. It is said that the chain alone was worth several pounds of pure gold. A large golden bangle adorned his wrist and another his elbow. An elaborately designed golden crown was put on his head, while his feet was adorned with ahenema sandals with intricate designs. Golden staff in hand, he was helped onto the special stool by the kingmakers. After holding court for a short time, he was now ready to be outdoored. The transformation was amazing. Once everything was ready, he was helped into his decorated palanquin; a young girl of about six years, Ebaekyi, also regally dressed, sat in front of him. Somiah, now Nana Ngoma II, held in one hand a bodua and in the other the ceremonial sword. As four strong porters carried him along the main streets of Aakonu, he danced in his palanquin, swaying the bodua and the ceremonial sword first to the left, then to the right, then resting both on his chest. This gesture is explained to mean that the left and the right of his chiefdom are one, and they belong to him. Two tall men held two large colourful umbrellas over his head which they kept spinning. The local band played joyful music as the procession continued from one end of Aakonu to the other. Food and drinks were in abundance. The partying went on throughout the weekend. It was an unforgettable experience.

Ebela

EGYA[4] AMAKYI HAD "PUT HIS MOUTH" on Ebela before she had even sprouted breasts. This happened when the new Chief of Aakonu, the beloved Nana Ngoma II made Ebela's father Egya Kodwo and Egya Amakyi elders of the stool. The elders were like the chief's cabinet. They helped him resolve disputes, advised him about critical issues, and generally served as his sounding board.

Before he agreed to become chief, Somiah had come to an agreement with the delegation that had come to seek him. He would be chief only if they allowed him to choose his own elders. They would advise him but the final decision would be his. The delegation agreed provided that he kept the people who were already in Ngoma I's cabinet. That was how younger men like Ebela's father, Egya Kodwo, got to be part of chief Ngoma II's elders' council.

Egya Kodwo had been delighted to be made a member of this elite group. The first meeting of the elders had run into late evening. Ebela's mother, Mokoa, had finished cooking and was

---

4   Egya is the Nzema word for "Mr." Aakonu is a village in Nzema.

waiting for her husband to return so she could serve him his dinner. There was no electricity in Aakonu and therefore no street lighting. It became dark once the sun went down. After waiting for some time, she sent young Ebela to the palace to find out when her husband would come home. The men had just gotten off their stools and were filing out of the Chief's compound when Ebela arrived. She went and stood quietly by her father as he said his goodbyes to the other men, one of whom was Egya Amakyi. Ebela curtsied and said good evening, all the while looking down at her feet as per custom. Egya Amakyi asked Egya Kodwo whether this was his daughter who a while ago was just a little baby on her mother's back. Her father said yes, she was, and how soon they grew up. Egya Amakyi then told him, "Kodwo, you have a beautiful daughter. She will make a lovely wife someday. I am telling you today I will marry her."

Ebela thought nothing of this brief encounter. Elderly men called young girls their wives all the time. At age eight she did not even know what that meant. But Egya Amakyi never forgot the request he had made. He asked Ebela's father about her every time they met, reminding him of his proposal of marriage and of the consent he had received. Not even Ebela's mother, Mokoa, had been told of this gentlemen's agreement to make her beautiful daughter the fourth wife of the venerable Egya Amakyi.

Egya Amakyi had been helping her father prosper ever since that proposal, supplying him with seeds to plant during the farming season, and providing for the expansion of his compound when he took on his second wife. Even three beautiful pieces of kente, the big sheep served at her puberty rites, and the metal trunk full of gold jewelry, quality cloth (asohyen), pomade, powder, soap, and ahenema sandals had been provided by Egya Amakyi. He had made sure his future wife was dressed and adorned in the best possible way. Egya Kodwo informed his wife Mokoa of Amakyi's marriage proposal and his agreement when two maidens from Egya Amakyi's compound delivered the package to their compound the week before Ebela's puberty rites. Mokoa was surprised, but at the sight of all the goodies, she figured that it was a testament to her and her husband's good parenting that someone as prominent as Egya Amakyi had been interested in her daughter, which was the best form of endorsement. Thus her initial anger at her husband was soon replaced by pride. Unfortunately, as was the case at the time, the person whose future had been decided had no idea about it.

To Ebela it happened too soon. In the few weeks since the puberty rites, she had been the talk of the village. The picture of her, glowing in her rich kente and accessories, her rich, dark, and well-oiled skin, her hair plaited neatly and wrapped in a beautiful headwrap (duku), her long, gazelle-like legs in ahenema sandals, could have adorned any magazine in the Gold Coast's department of tourism. The one thing she had looked forward to during her parade around the village with her friends was to see Mozu. She was relieved when they passed by the spot where he and his team were repairing their fishing net. The men had pretended to be preoccupied with their work as the girls passed. But Ebela had eyes only for one person. There was a brief moment when she turned around and met his gaze. For that moment the charade of busily working on the net was forgotten. Mozu, net and needle (agbuya) in his hands, had stared back at the beautiful Ebela. She held his gaze before realizing that the entire procession had stopped and was waiting for her to move forward.

One of the men remarked, "You look amazing Ebela. I hope Mozu brings you home soon." Mozu pretended to frown in the direction of the friend who made the comment. Then he turned and winked at her, as if to say, "You heard him, Ebela. I can't wait to take you home with me!"

This brought a smile on her face, a smile she held on to as the days went by, expecting him to come over with his family to ask for her hand in marriage.

The day Egya Amakyi's family came, she was home and had already finished her chores. They had finished having dinner unusually early. Her father said he had a meeting to attend at sundown. She had assumed that it was another meeting of elders at the chief's palace. But then they arrived and Ebela's younger brother opened the door and ushered them to the compound. Egya Kodwo's house is what one would call a "nouveau riche" in Aakonu. His large, walled compound had a gazebo-like structure in the main yard where he welcomed and entertained guests. Further away from the gazebo were several huts. One for himself, one for his wife Mokoa and her children, another for Ebela and her two siblings, and a third one for his second wife and her young son. The kitchen used by the two women stood beside the second wife's hut. The wives took turns to visit Egya Kodwo's hut on a weekly basis. As the first wife, Mokoa did not need any invitation to visit her husband's hut, except when he was there with her rival. She would go in whenever he was there alone and she had something pressing to discuss. The grounds of the compound were covered with beautiful coastal sand, which Ebela and her siblings kept impeccably clean by sweeping every morning and evening.

Her brother brought out a long bench for the visitors to sit on, then he went to call his father who was inside his hut getting himself ready. When Egya Kodwo came out, the men spent the first fifteen minutes in greetings, mentioning each other's achievements and titles, as was the custom. Two women in the entourage greeted Egya Kodwo and sat down, and the men continued praising each other until there were no more compliments to exchange. When the visitors had settled down, Ebela's father asked his brother, who was in the house at the time, to ask the *amanee*. Amanee was the way of finding out the purpose of a visit. It was so important, that any deviation from the correct procedure gave one a bad reputation. It would be said that he did not know *amamuo* (custom).

Ebela's uncle got up, greeted everyone once again and then started.

"It is well here. We woke up this morning safe and sound by the grace of the gods. As we all know, today being a Saturday we had to go to the sea. It is said that if a bird does not fly, it does not eat. As a result, we have gone to the sea and brought some food to eat. We have been hanging around here enjoying the breeze, until we were told we had visitors. So here we are, let us know why you are here, so that we can hide you in case anyone is after you to do you harm."

The use of proverbs in such gatherings was a given. The more proverbs a person used in speech, the wiser and more knowledgeable he or she was perceived to be. How else would these visitors and their host impress each other, if not through the use of proverbs?

Enu, a short, middle-aged man among the visitors, got up from his seat and adjusted his cloth. On such formal assignments, the men wore shorts, and a six-yard, high-end, printed cotton sheet wrapped around from the back, the loose ends coming over the left arm and tied in a knot. As Enu stood up, his knot came loose and he adjusted it, cleared his throat, and began. "We have heard you. We come in peace. As the elders say, an item of good quality sells itself. We are here on behalf of Egya Amakyi, our kinsman and your good friend and colleague on the chief's elders' council. He has seen a beautiful flower in your household. He has made enquiries and confirmed that this beautiful flower belongs to you. Therefore, he has sent us, his kinsmen, to come and formally express his interest in this flower. He knows that you will not disappoint him. So, in line with custom, and knowing his and your very good taste, he has sent us here with the best gin from abroad. This explains our visit."

Enu took his seat.

One of Ebela's cousins, a man of about twenty-five, stood up and addressed Ebela's father.

"Uncle and family members, thus says the delegation from Egya Amakyi's house. As the elders say, those who grind sweet spices do not clean their hands on the floor. Egya Amakyi has seen the good work done here by us, and his delegation is here as a testament to that. May I ask for your response?"

Egya Kodwo gestured to his nephew to come towards him. They had a short tête-à-tête. The young man got up again, cleared his throat, and continued.

"Agoo! My uncle says he has heard your request. It gives him great joy to have had an item good enough to have attracted Egya Amakyi's attention. He wants you to know that this is the best news he has heard in a long time. He accepts Egya Amakyi's request wholeheartedly. However, as the father of Ebela, he will have to deliver the wonderful news to his wife and her brothers, Ebela's uncles. He wants you to tell Egya Amakyi to expect a response by the next market day."

This was just what the delegation wanted to hear. They spent the next hour drinking local gin, eating cola nuts, and making small talk about the state of fishing, the gradual loss of the coastline, the changing weather patterns, the latest disease afflicting the coconut plants, and other such subjects. Finally, Enu sought permission on behalf of the guests to take their leave. Egya Kodwo granted them permission and they went away to report the outcome of their visit to Egya Amakyi.

Ebela and her mother were in the kitchen. They had watched the entire meeting through the holes in the kitchen wall. The kitchen and the entire compound had walls of raffia sticks. Such walls had narrow holes at the points where the sticks were tied together. The holes were small enough to keep insects out, but large enough to allow the breezes from the Atlantic to come through. Mokoa smiled to herself when she caught a glimpse of the people who had come to see her husband. Recalling what he had told her, she deduced right away that they had been sent by Egya Amakyi. But Ebela had no idea what was going on. When she saw the expression on her mother's face, she asked her why she looked so happy. Although her mother wanted to tell her, she knew it would be better to let her husband do so.

"Oh, I just remembered your mother Ezoma's invitation to her daughter's upcoming puberty rites. I am so excited about finally making the trip to see her after all these years," she responded.

"Oh yes, that will be exciting," Ebela agreed. Her mother Mokoa's older sister lived in Bokabo with her husband and three daughters. Ebela knew the middle daughter, who was about three months younger than her, was at the right age for her puberty rites. She had no reason to doubt her mother's response.

Ebela wanted to know badly the visitors' purpose. While her father received a lot of visitors, the dressing and formal mannerisms of the people who had come this time made her suspicious. She had recognized two of them as coming from Egya Amakyi's compound, but she never thought they would have come with a proposal of marriage. Maybe they had come on business—her father had a lot of dealings with Egya Amakyi. The man was almost sixty years old, with three wives and numerous children and grandchildren; Ebela was the same age as one of his daughters.

The work in the kitchen completed and the visitors gone, Ebela and her mother retreated to the main compound, where her excited father had just returned from seeing off the visitors. He called his wife over and told her what she had suspected. One can imagine how proud she was to hear the news. She, the mother of Ebela, would become the mother-in-law of the venerable Egya Amakyi. Considering how much they had enjoyed of Egya Amakyi's largesse, she could only imagine what they would receive when they were officially related. She recalled how Egya Amakyi had sponsored a cow at the funeral of his first wife Aso's mother. What a memorable funeral that was. The woman's coffin (eleka) was the most beautiful anyone had seen in the village. Only someone who loved you would give you such a burial. That funeral was still the talk of the town.

People in Aakonu believed a lot in the afterlife. A funeral was seen as the process by which the dead person made the journey to the other side to join the ancestors. Everything stopped from the day the person died to when they eventually got buried. Before the burial the person was dressed in their very best and laid in state. While lying in state, family members, friends and sometimes even strangers cried and sang dirges, extolling the good deeds of the deceased, how they would be missed, and why things would never be the same without them. The ability to sing the appropriate dirge to demonstrate your relationship with the deceased was considered so important that women (who usually sang the dirges) took time to learn it from their elders. After the burial came the rituals, when custom and precedent were followed religiously.

Family members who had neglected their roles in other funerals were named, shamed, and fined. The chief and his elders named the amounts of money that every family was expected to contribute towards the cost of the funeral. For someone like Egya Amakyi, the entire funeral became a spectacle, with food and drink in abundance.

Ebela still harboured a small suspicion about the visitors. But she could not bring herself to ask her father why they had come. After waiting for some time, she retired to bed.

She dreamt that the delegation had come from Mozu's family. The group of four, consisting of Mozu's two other fathers, Nyameke and Bonzo (his father's younger brothers), his mother's younger sister Avola, and his mother's brother Tayi brought five bottles of good quality gin and assorted valuables. She met them at the gate, brought out a bench for them to sit under the gazebo in the compound and went to find her father. She told him about the guests waiting in the compound. He came, exchanged pleasantries with the guests, and sat down to hear their mission. Contrary to what Ebela had expected, her father was not impressed with Mozu. Like many of his age, he did not trust the young men of the day. He thought them too unreliable, even when they were doing well. He loved his daughter too much to entrust her to an inexperienced man who might not be able to give her the security that a more elderly, self-made man would. Ebela had been watching her father's behaviour through the raffia walls of the kitchen; alarmed that he was going to reject the proposal of the man of her dreams, she run out and knelt before him and tearfully pleaded with him.

"Papa, please, I love Mozu. Please do not refuse his proposal. I love him so much. He is the one I would love to marry."

Egya Kodwo was scandalized. How could his daughter behave this way in the presence of the young man's emissaries? She was cheapening herself, when there were many suitors who would die for her. Ebela didn't care. As far as she was concerned, it was Mozu or nobody. Her father did not know what to say.

He led his daughter to the side of the kitchen, away from the guests.

"Mokoa!" he called out to his wife in anger. "Look at what your daughter is doing. Did you put her up to it?"

Mokoa run out of the kitchen to see what was going on.

"You'd better speak some sense to her. I will not tolerate this type of shameful behaviour from a daughter of mine." He left the two women standing by the kitchen and went inside his hut, away from the enquiring eyes of the guests. Mokoa looked at her daughter, and at the delegation waiting under the gazebo. Ebela was in tears. Mokoa knew what she needed to do. She entered her husband's hut where Egya Kodwo was pacing back and forth in anger.

"Kodwo, my husband," she pleaded with him. "You know your daughter as much as I do. There is little we can do to change her mind. Why don't we give her a chance?"

Eqya Kodwo knew his wife Mokoa very well. He remembered the many situations when he had listened to her advice, contrary to what many of her fellow men did, and she had been proven right. Sometimes he wondered whether or not she was not clairvoyant. Could this be one such situation? Ebela was his only daughter. Could he forgive himself if anything bad happened to her because of his foolishness?

Egya Kodwo reluctantly gave in, joined the delegation in the compound and accepted Mozu's proposal.

After a few more minutes of exchanging pleasantries, the group sought permission to leave.

Ebela was ecstatic. She thanked her father profusely before dashing back to the kitchen. She couldn't wait to finish her chores so she could go out and find Mozu to tell him the good news. There were also her best friends to share the news with.

Ebela met Mozu at the beach. They were locked in each other's arms the moment they met, oblivious of the fishermen repairing Mozu's father's fishing net nearby. Oh how they had been looking forward to this day! Finally, they would be with each other as man and wife. Ebela wondered aloud what it would be like to carry his baby. What kind of parents would the two of them make? How she would spoil that baby! Mozu, a man of few words, seemed unable to believe his lot. He had finally won the most beautiful girl in the village. The girl every boy, and even the older men, had been eyeing. He could not wait to take Ebela to his quarters in his father's compound. With his beautiful Ebela by his side, he could now say he had arrived. He would prove to her what a wonderful man he was. He would make sure that she and his future children never lacked anything.

Mozu wrapped his arms around her, admiring her beautiful frame, her silky hair tied up in beautiful braids, the beautiful wrapper that covered her breasts and her midsection, her waist adorned with beautiful beads. Ebela, who usually couldn't stand being touched, felt contented and happy with his every touch. She wished this day would never end.

But Alas! It happened so suddenly she had little time even to think. She turned around at a strange sound behind them, only to see a wave coming their way, the biggest wave she had ever seen. The sea had become a giant creature and snatched away the unsuspecting Mozu. Fear and anger took hold of her, and she lunged at the creature so hard that she felt her hand hit the floor and she was jolted out of her sleep. What a dream! How relieved she felt that nothing had happened to her beloved Mozu.

Two days passed since the delegation visited. Ebela had forgotten about it and was going about her business as usual. It was seven PM. She had cleaned the lanterns and was about to lie down to rest when her father called her.

"Mamekyi, Mame Ebela, come here."

Whenever he called her using that tone, it meant that he had something important to tell her. *Mamekyi* means "little mother." Egya Kodwo had named her after his mother's older sister. His own mother had died while giving birth to him, the ninth child. Of the nine, six had died in infancy. Only Egya Kodwo and his two brothers had survived. He was brought up by his mother's older sister, and she had done a great job at this. Whatever her biological children ate, these children ate. The boys never lacked anything. Even when their father remarried and forgot about them, she toiled hard to be able to take care of all of them. When Egya Kodwo started having his own children, he knew that he would have to name his daughter after his mother, Ebela. Since it is considered disrespectful to refer to an older person by their name, he would call his daughter Mamekyi, young mother, as a sign of respect and love for the person whose name he had given her.

Much could be said about names. A child had several names. There was a separate name associated with the order of the child's birth. The first-born child was called *fuamunli rale*, meaning a puberty child. Names like that did not usually become a child's regular name. Those that did were Mieza for a third consecutive boy, Assua for a seventh-born, or Nyameke and Nyonra for an eighth- and a ninth-born respectively.

There was a name based on gender and the day of birth (also called the soul name), each of which came with a nickname. In this context the "nickname" is used more for adulation than humour. For example, when an elder or a parent called a younger person by his or her nickname, it was usually to praise the person for achieving a feat or doing something worthy of praise. The gender based names often became regular names, especially when the father refused or was unable to name the child. A boy born on Saturday would be called Kwame, his nickname *Ato*, while a girl would be Ama, her nickname *Agyamalandu*. God was sometimes referred to in this village as *Nyamenle Kwame*, and Mother Earth, believed to be a girl born on Thursday, was *Azɛlɛ Yaba*. Yaba was the soul name for a girl born on Thursday, her nickname *Amele*, while a boy would be Kwaw, nickname *Ogonlo*. For the rest of the days, a boy born on Monday was Kodwo, nickname *Asela*, a girl would be Adwoba, nickname *Molesa*. A Tuesday born would be Kabenla, nickname *Abuo-Kabenla Bena-Woso* for a boy, while a girl will be Abenlema, nickname *Kwosia Animgbo*. Wednesday will be Kaku, nickname *Abaku* for a boy, and Akuba, nickname *Obologyi* for a girl. Friday will be Kofi, nickname *Abukofi* for a boy, and Afiba for a girl. Interestingly, and to the chagrin of many girls born on Friday, there does not seem to be a nickname for Afiba.

As the first-born and also born on a Sunday, Ebela could already lay claim to two names—she was fuamunli rale and also Akasi. The nickname for Akasi was *Ehiafo*. Her male counterpart would be Kwasi, nickname *Afum*. Ebela was called Akasi until she was six months old, when she was considered to be no longer at risk of dying. Then her father held a big naming ceremony during which he gave her the name Ebela, which was what everyone called her.

Ebela picked up a stool and went to her father. When he told her to sit down, she put the stool down and sat. Mokoa was already by his side. He cleared his throat and started: "Mamekyi, my daughter, I am sure you have been wondering what those people who visited me came for. I have been yearning to tell you. What has been holding me back is that I was waiting to hear from your mother's side of the family. You know that custom demands that I should get their agreement for any marriage proposal regarding you. Well, at long last, I have heard from them and they are all as excited as I am. The proposal was on behalf of Egya Amakyi."

Ebela opened her mouth but for a moment no word escaped. Then she said, "Egya Amakyi? What does he want, Papa?"

"You, of course," Egya Kodwo responded with pride. "Mamekyi, Egya Amakyi wants your hand in marriage, and I cannot describe how proud I am. You have made me proud!"

"No Papa, I am sorry. Egya Amakyi is too old. His youngest daughter is even older than me," Ebela broke into sobs. "I cannot possibly marry him, Papa!" She looked at her mother.

"Maame, can you tell Papa that I cannot marry Egya Amakyi?" Mokoa looked away, avoiding her gaze. Her father's temper began to rise. He tried to keep himself in check to reason with his daughter.

"Mamekyi," Mokoa began. "My daughter, you have made us so proud. You have no idea what this means to us. Egya Amakyi could have picked any other girl. Some of your friends who had their puberty rites before you have not yet been married. Those who have married are not having an easy time. Remember that friend of yours who ran away with that boy. You know what happened to her. We have been praying to the ancestors to send you a good suitor. Somebody who would be able to take very good care of you, and us. Our prayers have been answered. You should be happy, my daughter. Your father and I want the best for you."

Her father continued. "My daughter, pay heed to what your mother has just said. You should be very happy. Egya Amakyi has the means to take very good care of you and us. Do you know that the beautiful kente you wore was a gift from him? He has done a lot already and he has promised a lot more once you get married to him. We are happy for you, as you should be."

"Papa, Maame." Ebela looked at both of them. "I have heard you. Thank you for looking out for my happiness. But Egya Amakyi has three wives already. We know all the scary stories people tell about marriages with multiple wives. What if I do not get on well with the other wives? I am afraid of what would happen then."

Mokoa put her arms around her daughter protectively.

"Don't be worried, my daughter. Egya Amakyi's wives get on

very well with each other. Besides, as the younger one, you will be the favourite. He will make sure they take good care of you. Also, know that I will be right here. I am not going anywhere. So if anything comes up for which you need my advice, I will be just a compound away. Your father and I will not sit by and let you go into a marriage that will be bad for you. Trust us, my daughter. Everything will be fine."

There wasn't much Ebela could say at that point. Moreover, Mozu hadn't done anything to let her know whether he would be sending his people or not. As they say, a bird in hand is better than a thousand in the bush. She knew how well Egya Amakyi took care of his wives. It would not be so bad after all. Her parents were relieved when she told them she would marry him. Her father relayed the message to Egya Amakyi, who was overjoyed. Now all he had to do was to tell his current wives about this upcoming marriage. Not that they had a say in the matter. But for his own peace of mind and to make sure that there was harmony in his household, he had to tell them himself, rather than they find out from the street.

The next day Egya Amakyi called his wives one by one to his quarters, starting with his first wife Aso. He told them about Ebela, and his decision to make her his fourth wife. He assured them that her coming would not change anything with regard to their current arrangements. He still loved each of them dearly. What he asked for was for them to welcome her and treat her as their own daughter. He would not tolerate any behaviour from them that would bring his good name into disrepute.

Aso was both surprised and hurt. At this stage she was beginning to think that Amakyi would be slowing down rather than looking for another wife. She had known Amakyi long before he became so wealthy, and she was never shy of speaking her mind, as the two other wives were. Aso wanted to protest strongly, but she had nobody to back her, and so she resigned herself to concentrating on her business. And now that all the wives had been told, she knew there was nothing stopping him from bringing his new wife home.

The following Saturday was set as the day of the marriage.

Like her puberty rites, Ebela's marriage was the talk of the town. Nobody could make a lasting impression better than Egya Amakyi. For the marriage rites the groom was expected to bring a suitcase (called an "airtight") with at least three pieces of a six-yard high-end wax-print cloth, as well as golden necklaces, bracelets, and earrings, beads, saale, assorted types of powder and pomade, some amount of cash, and drinks. Egya Amakyi brought two dozen pieces of the high-end cloth and an abundance of the other items.

They were carried in the airtight and basins by six maidens. At the party, sheep, chicken, bowls full of fufu, rice, and other food were served. There were calabashes of palm wine, bottles of local and foreign gin, and crates of soft drinks. A popular band from Bokabo, a neighbouring village, was hired to provide music, which ranged from highlife to folk. Young drummers, clothed only round their waists, played on instruments of various sizes. The young and old danced. By the time the sun went down everyone was tired and drunk.

The celebrations over, the new bride, followed by her maidens and minders, made her way to Egya Amakyi's compound. She was welcomed wholeheartedly. She had her own room in the compound just like the rest of them. In the days that followed, the other wives took time to make her feel at ease, and she joked that she had three mothers now, in addition to the one she had left behind. If there was any discontent among them there was no sign of it. Before long she had settled into the routine of the compound. Each wife had a week with the husband.

But to Ebela it all felt absurd. Here she was, the wife of a man old enough to be her father. During their first night, she did not know what to do. Not even the crash course she had received during her puberty rites had prepared her for this awkward moment. She wondered if it would have been different with Mozu. Most definitely. The very thought of him did things to her body. Imagining the two of them holding hands and gazing into each other's eyes set her body on fire. How much more if she found herself beside him, touching him. She wouldn't have needed any guidance on what to do or where to touch. She felt that her body itself would have led the way. But she felt nothing with Egya Amakyi. She felt uncomfortable undressing before him, and insisted that they turn off the lantern. Egya Amakyi did not bother about making small talk, or even making sure that she was comfortable. He was not one to wait. Within minutes it was over, and he rolled over and was fast asleep. Ebela was left staring at the ceiling. "What just happened?" she asked herself, not expecting any answer. She remembered what one of her friends had said about her first time. It had been great. She wondered why her case was so ordinary. She cleaned herself, put on her wrapper and lay on the bed, trying to sleep. Would this be her new normal life? She felt nothing but disappointment at what she had settled for. Her thoughts of what it could have been with Mozu would forever remain a fantasy. It would be a retreat she would resort to whenever she had to endure this pretense of intimacy with Egya Amakyi.

The rest of her week was predictable. She took Egya Amakyi's food to him, she watched him eat while trying to make small talk, and then afterwards she would clear the bowls, freshen up, and go to sleep in his hut. He would come to bed, mount her, do his thing and fall asleep in minutes, leaving Ebela staring at the ceiling. She was relieved when the week was over.

If anyone benefitted from Ebela's marriage it was her parents. Their gamble had paid off in good measure. From the day he married their daughter, Egya Amakyi never stopped showering them with gifts of food, clothing, and provisions.

For about a month Ebela's activities were confined to the compound; she did not see anyone other than the people in Amakyi's household and those who came over either to congratulate her or to visit other members of the household. She wondered what would happen when she ventured outside. She yearned to find out how Mozu was doing. She could not get him out of her mind. The more she thought about him, the more she wondered what things would have been like. Would she be able to control herself when she saw him? Did he feel the same way about her, or was her imagination playing tricks on her? She wanted to tell her mother how she felt, but would her mother understand?

She knew from her mother's and grandmother's stories about marriages that they had not been about love. They had been marriages of convenience. It was not that they did not believe in love, they were simply pragmatic. Usually the young man you loved was finding his feet and not ready to settle down and start a family. For the young girls on the other hand, their parents were eager to marry them off, for fear that they could get pregnant and become burdens. This meant that they would rather have a well-established man marry her soon after puberty than let her sit around and "destroy" her life waiting for the one she loved.

One Wednesday afternoon, five weeks after Ebela's atofole (marriage ceremony), they heard the announcement from two young boys who worked for the *Sea Never Dry* fishing group, owned by Mozu's father, that their group had had a bumper catch. Along with the other fishing groups in Aakonu, *Sea Never Dry* had left at dawn.

Of the twenty-four men that made up the team of *Sea Never Dry*, the nine who paddled the canoe to sea were expert swimmers and did the most dangerous part of the work. They were called *Anwumama* or Upper people. For their reward, they received *abunsa*, or a third of the total revenue. A third of the revenue went to the owner of the canoe, in this case Mozu's father, while the remaining third went to the rest of the team, called the *Azeama* or shore men. While the Anwumama paddled the canoe out to sea, one of them would throw out one end of the rope. The fishing ropes used by the group was made of synthetic fibres twisted together into bundles to increase their overall length and tensile strength. A typical fishing group would have up to five knot-lengths of rope in their canoe when going out to sea. As the fishes were usually far out into sea, the fishermen tied the ropes to two sides of the net to allow it the needed length, one end pulled by the Azeama and the other by the Anwumama. As the canoe set off, the Azeama end of the rope would be thrown out, which someone would tie to a strong coconut tree as an anchor. Once the Anwumama found a school of fish, they would cast the net, make sure the fish had been trapped, then turn around and paddle ashore. They would tie their end of the rope to another anchor, and then both groups, now side by side, would pull the net in.

That dawn, like they had done on numerous occasions, the Anwumama group boarded the canoe loaded with their net and ropes.

"Tsooooooo boi!" the Azeama group cried as they pushed the canoe out into the water.

"Tsoooooooo boi!" responded the Anwumama group on board.

The captain, an astute fisherman named Kpole, sat at the helm with a long pole in hand, which he used to guide the canoe onto the oncoming wave. The rest of the Anwumama group, their paddles in hand and ready, rowed and rowed as the captain directed. They went up and down one big wave after another. As they went, Kakukyi, one of the young men in the canoe, gradually released the Azeama end of the rope. Azeama pulled what he let off, which they tied to a coconut tree to serve as the anchor.

Meanwhile Anwumama continued on in the canoe. The rope allowed the canoe to go up to ten kilometres out to sea if they needed to. On this day, when they had gone for about one and a half kilometers from the shore, they came across a school of herring and other fish and began to cast their net,

Once they were confident they had trapped the fish, they turned around and rowed back to shore in high spirits, singing excitedly as they rowed.

"Sisiw mbo!

Tabon mbo!

Sisiw mbo!

Tabon mbo!

Iyi ye adze a wøye a, ee

Iyi ye adze a wøye a, a a

Ofarnyi kwan tabon a,

Ommfa nnkø n'ekyir o

Sisiw mbo, Tabon mbo!

Sisiw mbo, Tabon mbo"

Translated loosely,

Thank you waist, Thank you paddle

Thank you waist, Thank you paddle

Is this something that is done?

Is this something that is done?

That when a fisherman paddles,
He doesn't paddle backwards.

Thank you waist, Thank you paddle
Thank you waist, Thank you paddle

Once ashore, they pulled their end of the rope and tied it to another strong coconut tree just like the Azeama had done earlier.

The two groups were now on the shore, about two hundred metres apart. Each group pulled its portion of the fishing rope, walking backwards, and singing at the top of their lungs. When the net was about two hundred metres away from the shore, two men, one from the Azeama group and the other from the Anwumama group, were dispatched to go and guide the net to the shore. They walked alongside it as their colleagues continued to pull the ropes, ensuring that there were no holes in it to allow the fish to escape. When the net was finally pulled to the shore the elated fishermen screamed in excitement. The fishing net was so full they needed reinforcement to prevent it from tearing. Two young men, Amande and Nyanzu, were sent to go and announce that *Sea Never Dry* had landed a big catch.

That was when Ebela went to see what was happening at the shore and buy fish for dinner. She wore just the right combination of clothes to show her status as a new bride. A custom-made top (kaba) made from the coveted Vlisco wax print, over a one-piece slit (long skirt) of the same wax material which covered her legs and waist. She folded another piece of the same wax print and left it loosely over her shoulder. She wore earrings, a chain, and a bracelet, and her hair was wrapped in a scarf in a way that enhanced her beautiful face. She had a look of a goddess. People stopped to greet and congratulate her so that she was delayed reaching the canoes.

When she finally got there they had finished selling the smaller fish and were negotiating the prices of the bigger ones. She was only interested in some big fish for the day's dinner; after considerable haggling, she finally got what she needed. She said goodbye and set off for home, disappointed that she had not seen Mozu. Could he be sick? Or had he avoided her? She had not asked anyone about him for fear of arousing suspicion. The least suspicion could put them both at risk. On the way she decided that since she had a bit of time on her hands, she would pass by the riverside to search for periwinkle snails. These tiny creatures were both tasty and good for health and considered a delicacy. She could not go into the mangrove in her outfit, however, and decided therefore to scour the riverbed for stray ones.

She did not expect anyone to be there at this time, and definitely not any of the fishermen. They would all either be by their nets where the fish were being sold, or by the canoes preparing for the next day. And so she was startled to hear a whistle behind her. She turned around and to her amazement, standing behind a young coconut tree was Mozu. Her Mozu. She would not have seen him if he had not whistled. She was not sure how to react and stood frozen in her tracks. Mozu chuckled.

"Ebela, or should I call you Mrs Amakyi?" he teased.

He wore the shorts he had gone to sea with and a faded sleeveless undershirt, a singlet. He had been swimming while the fish were being sold. He was wet from head to toe, and his clothes clung to his body. His broad chest looked like it was ready to burst free from the light covering he had on. His frame alone was a rock of confidence. Ebela could not help but stare at this mountain of masculinity standing in front of her.

"What does it matter, Mozu? You can call me whatever makes you happy. But what are you doing here when you should be working on your net?"

"I came here to be away from everyone. Ebela, I haven't been myself since you married Amakyi. I come here every day after the net is down just so I can be alone and clear my head." He paused, expecting her to rebuke him. After all, he had only been admiring her from a distance. He had never really had the guts to declare his love for her. Why did he expect her to seek his permission before marrying?

"I know what you are going to say. I had not done anything to let you know that I love you, and wanted to marry you. I am sorry, Ebela. Seeing you get married to someone else has really hit me hard. I did not think it would affect me this way."

Ebela felt sorry for him. Why couldn't they have found a way to show each other what they felt? If she had known he loved her, like he was saying, she would have done everything she could not to agree to marry Egya Amakyi.

"Mozu, I love you too. I love you so much. But I never knew whether you felt the same way about me. Why didn't you tell me something? You have known me all this time. Why?" She half asked and half implored him.

He had come to stand close behind her. His towering frame engulfing her, Ebela felt secure in his presence. She could have melted into his arms.

Mozu turned her around to face him, his eyes looked longingly into hers. She had to raise her head to be able to keep his gaze. "Ebela, my dear, I have only myself to blame. Every time I tried to tell you, I felt this big lump in my throat. It was almost like I got possessed. All the words I had spent time rehearsing just abandoned me. You have no idea how many times I watched you draw water from the well or followed you as you went to gather firewood, but never had the strength to show myself and tell you how much I loved you. Remember the day you spoke my name during the Anyima song?"

Ebela recalled that moment vividly. "Yes," she responded with nostalgia. "Where were you? Did you really hear me say your name or did someone tell you?"

"I heard you myself. I was with the guys pretending to play hide-and-seek. We were not concentrating on our game. We were listening for our names. We could hear you but you girls could not see us because it was dark. I almost melted when I heard you mention my name."

"Well then, Mozu, why didn't you use that as a clue that I was in love with you?"

"Ebela, you did mention this other guy as well in subsequent songs. How could I know whether you really meant it when you mentioned my name? You know how many other guys felt about you. We were always left guessing who was winning in your books."

Ebela smiled to herself. She remembered very well. She had not wanted to seem like she was throwing herself at him. She had mentioned the guys she did not care anything about, just so that she would not seem too "out there," the one doing the chasing.

There was one unspoken rule in Aakonu when it came to relationships. A girl must never be known to be the one doing the chasing. The boy was expected to be doing everything possible to get her. The girl was expected to play hard to get. The same rules applied when it came to marriage. Even if the man had nothing and the woman was swimming in money, it must be the man who paid the bride price. Any offer by the woman to help or make the payment would be construed as being cheap or the man not being a complete man. This meant Ebela could not have done anything that would be seen as professing love for Mozu.

That was all in the past now.

Here they were, under a coconut tree with only the river in front of them. Ebela knew there was no way she would have the strength to resist if Mozu tried anything with her. At this moment she did not really care about the consequences, but later there would be a huge price to pay. A newly married woman in a compromising situation with a man would be the topic of all the gossips in the town. If they were found doing anything sexual, both would be stripped naked and paraded around the village. It would be an abomination with far-reaching consequences that would last generations. Mozu would be banned from the community. And there were the many gods roaming around them, looking for bad behaviour. They would have a field day, afflicting them with all kinds of diseases.

But she did not have time to think about all that. If only she could melt into him and the two of them ran away to a faraway land. Just the two of them and however many children they would have.

Mozu loved her too much to inflict any such consequence on her. For now he was content just holding her. Staring into her eyes. Telling her how much he loved her. He would always be there for her. She should never think that she had nobody. And if ever she became available he would not waste time.

They held on to each other for a long time. They did not need words to tell each other what they felt. When they finally let go of each other it was late afternoon. Ebela needed to get home to make dinner. Mozu looked around to make sure they were not seen, then said goodbye to Ebela as she took her basin of fish and periwinkle snail and set off for home. He watched her till she was out of sight. He was glad he had been able to control himself. He wouldn't have forgiven himself if anything happened to Ebela because of him.

Ebela was still in a trance when she got home. She could not believe her luck. She had finally heard from Mozu what she had been dreaming about all the time. Knowing that he loved her was exhilarating. His promise to be there for her was even more reassuring. And she was grateful that he had been able to control his desire. She would not have been able to resist if he had tried to go further with her. She felt very good. It did not matter anymore that Amakyi was not Mozu. All she needed to do was picture Mozu holding her and she would bear anything.

It was three months since the wedding. She had been following how well Mozu's father's net had been doing lately. She knew that Mozu had stopped going to sea and was helping out on the shore. He spent a lot of time alone by the river. He loved to swim. Being in the river was like therapy for him. Ebela knew that she had something to do with his state of mind. If only she could be with him. She knew however that the next time she was with him they might not be able to control their desires. They could be seen, so for her own sanity and for his sake she stayed away from him while doing everything to follow how he was doing.

One late Sunday afternoon, Ebela was on her way to visit her mother at her house when she met Ndabia, Mozu's close friend; he was leaving her father's compound. Ndabia had grown up in the same compound as Mozu. They were of the same age and were teammates on *Sea Never Dry*. He knew of his friend's secret crush on Ebela, and how hard her marriage had been on him.

"Madam Amakyi, is that you? So good to see you," Ndabia greeted her, bowing as if he were greeting an elder. Ebela heard the sarcasm.

"Ndabia, it's good to see you too. What happened? I haven't seen you in a while," she said. "Don't tell me your friend Mozu sent you here to torment me!"

"Well, he did not," Ndabia replied matter-of-factly.

"What brings you here then?"

"I have a message for your father, which is why I came to see him. And by the way, Mozu told me his father has suggested to him that he get married to cure him of his boredom. So, in case you hear anything about that, remember I told you first."

"And what did he say to his father?"

She could hardly compose herself, but she could not show Ndabia she still yearned for Mozu.

"Madam Amakyi," Ndabia made sure to emphasize her new name. "Why would you care what he said to his father?" He waited for her to respond but she had nothing to say.

"Since you seem to care so much, I might as well tell you. From what he said he told his father, it does not look like he is ready to get married anytime soon."

Ebela felt relieved. It took everything in her to keep herself from almost jubilating in Ndabia's presence.

She bid Ndabia goodbye and the two parted company, she to her father's compound, and he to his house. Ndabia had sensed that she still cared about his friend. He made sure to relay the outcome of their encounter to Mozu.

Ebela had not been feeling well lately. She had been using herbs to treat her fevers, but she did not improve. It was as though her system was fighting to keep out food. The very smell of food made her nauseous. One of the women in the house finally asked her,

"Ebela, are you pregnant?"

Ebela was surprised.

"Why do you ask?"

"You look pale. What you have is called morning sickness. It usually happens when you are pregnant. When was your last period?"

Ebela was embarrassed. She couldn't remember the exact date, but it was a while back.

The woman spoke to her at length, advising her what she needed to do, what to eat, and how to carry herself.

Ebela thought hard. Could she really be pregnant? Would she be a mother soon? What gender would her child be? She would like to have a girl. She would enjoy dressing her up and braiding her hair, just like how her own mother Mokoa used to do for her. She would give her everything she had and more. Her mother would be happy too. Which mother wouldn't be happy at the thought of having a granddaughter to carry on the family line? In their matrilineal culture, children belonged to their mother's clan, or *abusua*. Ebela's children would belong to the Alɔnwɔba clan, like her. Daughters ensured the expansion of a clan. It was believed that each clan had descended from a female ancestor. Each clan was symbolized by a totem; the Alɔnwɔba clan's totems were a falcon and a raffia palm.

Along with the totem, there are also specific qualities that are associated with each clan. People of the Alɔnwɔba clan are known for their statesmanship, bravery and patience. The Ndwea clan has a dog and fire as its totems, and honesty, industriousness as the qualities of Ndwea people. The Ezohile, another clan, has three totems – a cat, a crow and rice. They are also associated with rain. They are the opposite of Ndwea. For their qualities, Ezohile people are known for their statesmanship and their patriotism. Nvavile clan's totems are a parrot and corn. People of the Nvavile clan are known for their eloquence. The Adahonle clan's totems are an Eagle and palm. For their qualities, people of the Adahonle clan are known for their calmness and patience. The

Azanwule have the buffalo and yam as their totems, and honesty and uprightness as their qualities. The Asamangama, also known as Mafolɛ, are known for their bravery and aggressiveness. Their totems are the Panther and gold. Mafolɛ are associated with wealth.

These totems are displayed prominently during funerals. So much is made of these clans and their qualities that it sometimes features prominently in matchmaking decisions. Sometimes, during fundraisers and community team building activities clans compete among themselves for bragging rites as well.

Ebela did not know what to feel. What if her baby was a boy? Amakyi would be thrilled. It would make her even more favoured among the wives. Amakyi had four other sons, two of whom were already married, with kids, and the other sons were almost ready to marry. Another son would provide a good opportunity for him to re-live his youth.

Ebela wanted a child, yes. Wasn't that what should happen after the atofole? Still, she wasn't sure. Having Amakyi's child would make the prospect of being with Mozu even slimmer. How long would she be able to keep up her charade of being married to one man while yearning for the embraces of another? Mozu might decide to marry, knowing that being with her was unthinkable after she had Amakyi's child.

The sound of a co-wife calling her name made her snap out of her daydream. Should she tell her? But nobody announced their pregnancy in Aakonu. People simply found out. It was very much the next step after the marriage ceremony, so there was nothing to tell and no explanation was required. She would tell her mother at least. Her mother would advise her what she needed to do to ensure a healthy pregnancy.

It turned out she didn't even need to worry about that. Every morning women visited their neighbours to greet them and find out how they were doing. If the person had done something for them the previous day, then it was even more imperative to go and "thank them properly." Her mother came by to check on her and to thank her husband for the gifts he had sent them the previous day. Ebela was sweeping the compound when her mother arrived. She put the broom away and, after the usual traditional lengthy greeting, offered her a seat. Before sitting down, her mother took a good look at her and asked: "Ebela my daughter, you look pale. Are you pregnant? When was the last time you had your period? Have you been having morning sickness?"

Ebela wasn't sure how to answer.

"Maame, are you done? Which question do you want me to answer first?"

Her mother responded jokingly, "Answer them whichever way you choose."

"Maame, I have been having morning sickness for some time now, and I haven't seen my period in a while. My sister-in-law thinks I am pregnant, but as you can see, my stomach is still very small."

She touched her stomach lightly, and her mother smiled.

"You have made me so happy. You are pregnant, my daughter, and I can't wait to welcome and spoil my grandchild."

Mokoa looked lovingly at her daughter, already thinking of all the things she would do with her grandchild.

"Ebela, you know how people can get jealous of your good fortune and try to harm you spiritually. I would not be a good mother if I did not get you protected. All kinds of things happen to pregnancies in this village. I will not just sit here and let anything happen to you. Get ready. I will come this evening, and we will go and see Priestess Yaba. She will give you medicines to protect you." Ebela nodded.

That evening just after six her mother arrived, bringing a packet of candles and a bottle of Florida water perfume. The two women set off for Priestess Yaba's compound. A resident patient welcomed them at the gate and led them to the shrine where the Priestess was sitting in her Sesegua. They removed their slippers and lay prostrate at her feet. She took the jug of Florida water from the shrine and sprinkled the perfumed water on them. She asked them to get up and take a seat. When they had sat down, she asked them what had brought them. Ebela's mother replied.

"Our mother, we are here this morning because we have good news. Our daughter Ebela, with whom my husband and I were blessed, thanks to your prayers, is herself with child. We have brought her here to inform you and to thank you, and also to ask for protection for her to have a safe pregnancy."

Mokoa lay the packet of candles and the bottle of perfume before her. Priestess Yaba looked intently at the mother and daughter. She recited some incantations and said,

"You have come well, my daughter. The gods are pleased with people who show appreciation for their work. They have told me to assure you that what you have requested is not beyond them. Ebela here is their daughter, and they will make sure that she is safe."

She began shaking and fell into a trance. Her eyes rolled as if turning inside her head. All the while she was speaking in what sounded like gibberish to the two women. After what seemed like a long interval, she came out of her trance. Then she addressed them again.

"Ebela, this is what the gods say. You should not eat any fresh fish, and you are not to visit the communal well. You will be coming here every evening to bathe in a special concoction that I will make for you. I will give you special bracelets and anklets made of red and white calico and beads. You will put one on every joint of your legs and arms. They will keep you and your baby safe."

The two women went home, relieved that Ebela and her unborn baby were from now onwards under the protection of the venerable Priestess Yaba. Every evening Ebela went to the compound (the garden) of the priestess to rinse in the blessed water. She took care that no fresh fish was cooked in her utensils, for fear that she might unknowingly eat food from them. This was how seriously people took the priestess's instructions. Who would dare disobey, when there were many examples of people who faced grave consequences for not obeying the instructions they were given to the letter? There was the example of Priestess Yaba herself. The story is told that when the gods chose her to be their mouthpiece, they first attacked her mother Soma with a form of epilepsy. During the divinations the revered priestess at the time, Priestess Ehwia, indicated to Soma that the gods wanted her daughter Yaba to be their priestess. Soma was not too keen about this, fearing that once her only child became a priestess, she would not give her any grandchildren. She sent her daughter to live with her sister in Obuasi. She had forgotten that the gods were not limited by distance. Soma's epilepsy became worse until finally she gave in and sent for her daughter to come and start her tutelage under the Priestess Ehwia. Although her condition improved, she suffered a heart attack and died soon afterwards. The belief was that the gods had punished her.

Ebela's pregnancy progressed without any issues. She avoided Mozu so he would not see her pregnant. Fortunately, most men can't tell when a woman is pregnant until she is fully out. Ebela also wore bigger cover clothes as her condition became more pronounced, and she made sure not to go out so often during the day in case she ran into him. But she kept up with news about how he was doing, and if he had taken an interest in any other girl.

Things started to change after six months into her pregnancy. First her feet got so swollen she could hardly walk. Then she suffered shortness of breath. The least amount of activity made her dizzy and ready to faint. Her stomach had become considerably bigger, so much so that she felt as though she were rolling on the floor when she walked. This only served to make her depressed. There was so much going on in her mind, with no one she could trust enough to confide in. She became irritable, especially around Amakyi. He and his other wives all brushed this off as a side effect of the pregnancy and did everything to accommodate her. She only became worse.

The priestess advised her to come live in her compound. She moved there with her mother. Once there she had to rinse herself in the blessed water morning and evening. The following two months were difficult. She could only rely on what the priestess said. They offered countless sacrifices and performed several cleansing rituals, but to no effect.

One afternoon, when she went behind the yard to take her enema, her waters broke. She had been feeling terrible lower-back pains, hence her decision to use the enema. She cried out for her mother, who ran up and helped her back into the compound. The priestess checked and confirmed that this was the onset of labour. While they were not trained to deliver babies, most priestesses acquired this skill through practice, having been initiated by their older colleagues. After a few hours of labour, the priestess realized that Ebela's was not going to be a normal delivery. By midnight, after some twelve hours, Ebela delivered a baby girl. To everyone's surprise, the priestess pronounced that there was one more in there. Ebela had been carrying twins all the while. However, she also saw something that made her look worried. The second baby was presenting with its legs first. Ebela was fatigued and had lost a lot of blood. The priestess had no experience of handling such a case. By the next morning a weakened Ebela could hardly keep her eyes open. More sacrifices were made for the safe delivery of the remaining twin and the placenta. But nothing seemed to work.

That afternoon, a team of health officials from WestBay, the regional capital, happened to be visiting Aakonu for an assessment when they heard about Ebela in the priestess's compound. They dispersed the crowd that had gathered inside the compound and got down to work. The curious crowd moved back and regrouped to watch, wail, and gossip. After several nail-biting hours, the health officials delivered a baby boy, but he was dead. Meanwhile Ebela had gone into a coma.

The village was thrown into mourning; people thought they had lost both Ebela and her baby boy. Amakyi did not know what to do with himself. As for Mokoa, the very sight of her was enough to break people's hearts. Amidst this grief, a girl of fourteen had started screaming and shaking hysterically. It could be seen that she was possessed. She was taken to Priestess Yaba, who then began to interrogate the girl.

"Who are you?"

The girl danced around in circles. She stopped suddenly, looked intently at the priestess. People had gathered, all eyes were on her. She opened her mouth as if to speak, then turned and danced around again, this time at a faster pace. She stopped, and the priestess asked a second time: "Who are you?"

The girl laughed hysterically and said, "I am the wife of the god of Amanzule River. Why are you all so sad? Is it because of her?" She pointed to the room where Ebela lay in coma. "I have come for her. She was given to me. Yaba thinks she is strong. She thought she could keep me from taking what is mine. No, not this time. I have her now."

"Who gave her to you?" Priestess Yaba asked.

"Hahahaha," another hysterical laugh. "You expect me to tell you? No, and you can't make me," she responded cheekily.

With this, the girl gave a loud shriek and fell to the floor. The Priestess asked the crowd to leave her alone. After a few minutes she got up and looked around sheepishly. The people were not surprised, such things happened. Nobody asked if the girl was actually possessed or had merely pretended, nobody could tell. She was led home by her mother.

The city medical team attended to Ebela throughout the night until she regained consciousness the next morning. There was relief all around that at least she had pulled through, though the baby had died. He was buried in the evening. Ebela was in a daze. When she refused to see or hold her surviving daughter, everyone knew something was wrong. She would not stop talking to herself, mentioning Mozu's name and asking where he was.

"Where is Mozu?" she asked her mother. "I want to see him. Why is he hiding from me? Did that child have anything to do with Mozu's absence? I don't want to have anything to do with her. She is not mine. I want Mozu. Where is he?"

Mokoa did not know what to do. She put her hand on Ebela's mouth to shut her up, in case someone heard her and became suspicious about what really was the cause of her sickness. Ebela would not shut up. She pushed her mother's hand away. At one point she became so agitated she pushed her mother with such strength that the older woman fell against the wall. Priestess Yaba called on others to help restrain her. They sent for her father and Amakyi. The two men came right away, but the moment she set eyes on Amakyi, Ebela became even more agitated.

"Go away from me, Amakyi. I do not want to see you. What are you doing here? Make him go away!" She screamed, looking at her father.

"Calm down, my daughter," he said. "It is us. It is Amakyi. He is your husband, he means you no harm."

"No, I do not know him. I have nothing to do with him. I want Mozu. Get me Mozu!"

Egya Kodwo could not believe his ears. He was too ashamed even to look at Amakyi. The latter was justifiably annoyed. He stormed out of the compound. Egya Kodwo knew his daughter was not her usual self. Else, how could a new mother refuse to touch, let alone feed her own baby? Someone must have placed a curse on her. His only hope was that Priestess Yaba would be able to help cure her soon enough before he lost his daughter. He knew Amakyi had every right to be angry. He would be too, if he were in his shoes.

The people of Aakonu had already made up their minds. Someone had cursed Ebela. Someone who wanted to harm her and her baby. But who could that possibly be? Who stood to benefit should Ebela and her baby fail to survive? All eyes fell on Aso. She was Amakyi's first wife but had nothing to show for it. All her pregnancies had ended in stillbirth or death, not counting numerous miscarriages. For her to sit there and watch the latest wife, who not too long ago was a little girl herself, successfully give birth to not one but two babies would be embarrassing and painful. That was how the rumour that Aso had used her witchcraft to make Ebela sick in the head started. Some went as far as saying that but for the strong power of Priestess Yaba, Aso would have killed even Ebela's remaining baby and Ebela herself through her witchcraft.

To those making these allegations against Aso, it didn't matter that she had welcomed Ebela to their home and treated her like her own child. It didn't matter that she had stood up for Ebela when her other rivals and sisters-in-law had tried to cheat her out of her allowance or her farming plot. Nobody let their children eat from Aso's pot lest she harm them through a spell. This isolation had pained her. Life in a village is harsh. People draw conclusions, especially on issues related to the spiritual, often without a shred of evidence. A woman in her sixties with no living offspring is an easy target for people looking for someone to blame for their misfortunes, to accuse of witchcraft. People pointed at her behind her back. It became unbearable. The more she became depressed and felt isolated, the more she withdrew into herself, so that people became even more convinced that she was a witch. The once vibrant, industrious Aso became a shadow of herself. It was only a matter of time before Amakyi would use her condition as grounds for divorce.

Meanwhile, Mozu had heard what was going on with Ebela. Out of respect for her, and in order not to aggravate the situation, he stayed away, but he made sure that his friend Ndabia kept him informed. He had to play his cards right. He was relieved that he had not done anything improper with her that could have displeased the gods. But if only there was something he could do.

When Ebela's condition made no progress over a month, Priestess Yaba discharged her. But Ebela did not want to go to Amakyi's compound. Egya Kodwo took her to his compound. If anyone from Amakyi's compound approached her, she would throw a violent tantrum. She would not have anything to do with her baby. Caring for Ebela and her baby took a toll on Mokoa.

One day the situation became truly unbearable. Ebela had become aggressive and was about to strip herself naked. She would not eat or sleep unless she saw Mozu. What had they done with him? Why were they keeping him away from her? Had Amakyi killed him already? She had to be where Mozu was. She would hit anyone who came close to her, unless it was Mozu. Mokoa was very convinced that getting Mozu to visit Ebela would be their only answer at that point. She pestered Egya Kodwo about inviting him for a visit.

Egya Kodwo finally relented. What could they lose by inviting Mozu over? If that would help heal his daughter, then so be it. He sent his nephew to tell Mozu and his father what was happening, and ask if Mozu would be so kind as to come and see his daughter.

When the nephew arrived with the request, Mozu's father was relaxing in his verandah. He said he would find Mozu and send him over. He had not seen much of his son lately. He knew that he was preoccupied about something. Now he knew what it was. The once lively Mozu had withdrawn into himself and preferred to be by himself, usually by the river where he swam or pretended to catch crabs. The change in him was like night and day.

Mozu's father went to look for his son. As expected, he found Mozu by the riverside, staring at nothing in particular. It seemed like he had a lot on his mind.

"Mozu, my son," his father said. "I was told I would find you here, and here you are. How have you been?"

Mozu stood up and walked towards his father.

"I am doing all right, father. I am just worried about Ebela and all that is going on."

"I came here to find you because they want you to go to their house."

"No, Father, I cannot possibly go there. That would not be wise. You should know that."

"My son, I would have to disagree with you on this. Her father sent for you because, as I understand, her situation is very bad. She has refused to eat or do anything until she sees you. It is important that you go to her. Everybody will know that you went there to try and help. It was not for anything else."

The two men walked to Ebela's family compound together. His father left once they arrived. Ebela was sitting on a stool in front of her mother's hut. As soon as she saw him she ran and embraced him.

"Mozu, is that you? Is that really you?" she asked. Turning his head from side to side as if to make sure that he was real.

"Yes, Ebela. It is me," Mozu replied, disentangling himself and feeling very embarrassed.

"I am so glad. I thought Amakyi had killed you. Mozu, you have no idea how scared I have been."

From the way she was talking, it did not appear that she had become so violent only a short time ago that she had to be restrained. Mokoa, Egya Kodwo, and everyone else who was in the yard stared at her in disbelief. Mozu held her gently till they reached her stool. He helped her sit down and then he sat on the ground by her side. Ebela removed the stool from under her and also sat down on the ground, resting her body against his. She looked peaceful. They sat there for over an hour, and finally she fell asleep. Her parents helped him put her on her bed, then he asked leave of them and left. He assured her parents that he would return the next day. This was the first time in several days that she had gone to sleep without a struggle. If they had any doubt what effect Mozu would have on her recovery, it was long gone.

The next few weeks Mozu came around every day. He got her to eat and take a bath. He even got her to hold her baby a few times without trying to harm her. Most times they did not say a word to each other. She would just sit by him, resting her head on his shoulder. Once in a while she would lift her head up to look at him, as if to reassure herself that he was real and that he was still there. Amakyi could not accept this situation and divorced her. He took his daughter, whom he named Aso, after his first wife. Ebela agreed that Aso should be the one to bring up her daughter. She knew that in spite of what people said, Aso was a wonderful woman, just the right person to raise her daughter.

Mozu devoted himself to nursing his love back to good health, and finally formally asked for her hand in marriage.

Ahu: Love and Loss

ANOTHER JOLT OF PAIN THROUGH my lower body brought
me out of my daydream back to reality. My fourth delivery was
proving more difficult than I had thought possible. Nana had yet
to return from her visit to Priestess Yaba. From the two women
attending to me I had heard that the Priestess had requested a
bottle of perfume and twenty-five shillings in addition to the initial list of items. Twenty-five shillings was the equivalent of one
American dollar. As the pain tapered off, my mind wandered
again to the time when I got married to my first husband. After
what seemed like a long time following Ebela's and my puberty
rites, Homiah, a young man from Sanvoma, some fifty kilometres
west of Aakonu, came to ask for my hand. He was about twenty-
two years old, of medium height, rather slim but athletic looking
and with a calm demeanor. I would have preferred to have married someone in Aakonu. Sanvoma was not too bad either, except
that girls in Aakonu did not like to marry "strangers."

Who in Aakonu did not know the story of the young woman
who went away with a stranger and almost never made it? She was
a very beautiful girl and refused all suitors from her own village

and even the neighbouring ones. Simple and learned, rich and poor, young and old, she refused them all. Neither her parents nor anyone else could convince her to accept someone. She became known as a snob. It turned out that a python heard about her and decided to teach her a lesson. It changed itself into a handsome young man and visited her village. He met the girl at the edge of the river as she was drawing water. She was so smitten by his looks that she accepted to marry him right away. She could not wait for him to pay her bride price. Her parents advised her to wait until she knew more about him but she refused. When they would not accept her bride price, which he finally offered, because it was too low, she threw the money at them and ran off with him. As they journeyed through the forest, the path kept closing behind them. They walked for three days, during which the nice and handsome stranger changed completely in his behaviour. He would not wait for her to catch up and only responded to her with grunts and monosyllables. The farther they journeyed, the more irritable he became. On the third day, he stopped by a small stream and asked her to wait for him. When he emerged, he was not the handsome young man she had followed but a mean-looking python. She was terrified, but there was nowhere for her to go. The python started to swallow her. She begged and screamed for help, but there was no one else around. He had almost swallowed her when out of nowhere flew an arrow; it hit the snake and killed it. It had been shot by a hunter from her village, whom she had previously refused to marry. He was in the bushes nearby when he heard her screams. He helped her to get back home, where she narrated her scary ordeal to all.

And so with this story in mind, I accepted Homiah's proposal. He was known by most people in Aakonu, since he had played for Sanvoma in soccer, oware, and other competitions against Aakonu.

I was more than happy to be gone, given that most of the girls my age had already been married. I was my husband's first wife. Like most young men in Sanvoma he was a fisherman. Sanvoma is also along the coast; in every way Sanvoma is just like Aakonu, but without the famous Amanzule River, which takes its source from a lake about twenty kilometres north of Sanvoma. There were two fishing groups in Sanvoma, the Eagles and the Sanvoma Boaters. Homiah was a key member of the Sanvoma Boaters. He was part of the Anwumama group, those who took the canoe to the sea, a coveted position he held by virtue of his strong physique and swimming ability. As a result, he got abunsa. This meant my husband did very well during the fishing season, earning about double what his colleagues who were not part of the Anwumama group made. During the off season he helped maintain the net, and also worked on a small piece of land on which we had a sizable cassava farm. He had a modest compound next to his father's where we stayed. In three years of marriage we had two children, a boy and a girl of whom I was very fond.

A few months after our second child was born, the unexpected happened. It was a beautiful day in April, at the height of the fishing season. The team had gone for the usual shift and gotten a very sizable catch. They had finished selling to the women and were ready to prepare the canoe, ropes and nets for the next day when they spotted a large school of fish in the ocean. To the trained eye a school of fish can be spotted miles out to sea just from the behaviour of the waves. Once it was confirmed that this was really a potentially big catch, the men got to work. They called out the regular Anwumama, and within minutes the canoe was ready to go. Off they went, the nine regulars, with Homiah, my husband at the helm. They had gone about a mile out and were in the process of laying the net when the skies suddenly changed. Heavy winds arrived with rain and huge waves, creating total chaos. The wooden canoe was no match for the waves and the winds. It overturned, and the men tried desperately to hold on to the overturned canoe as the waves and the rain attacked them. Nobody noticed that Homiah was still under the canoe. He had been at the helm, therefore everyone assumed that he would be the first one out, especially since he was an accomplished swimmer. But he had gotten entangled in the nets under the capsized boat and couldn't get out. News of the accident spread, the entire village was on edge. People feared the worst. I had run home from the farm at the first sign of the rain and made it just in time before the winds set in. I put firewood into the *mokyea* and was fetching fire from my brother-in-law's kitchen when I heard the wailing in the compound.

"Ahu, Ahu, have you heard?" Nyevile, a young woman from the next compound called out to me. "They say Homiah and his crew are still at sea, and their canoe has capsized."

I almost dropped the glowing charcoal on my foot.

"What? They just finished selling the catch, why are they still at sea?"

"It seems they went a second time, before the winds started."

I was shaken, but I thought that Homiah was a great swimmer and would survive. My only concern was for any new member who might be in danger—as the captain it would fall on Homiah to make sure they were safe. Although Anwumama were all accomplished swimmers, sometimes when conditions looked good they went to sea with younger members who showed promise.

The news also spread to the nearby villages on the coast. Much as everyone was eager to help, they had to wait for the winds to settle enough for them to be able to reach the stricken canoe and the men. There were no outboard motors, therefore the rescuers would have to paddle rescue boats to reach the overturned canoe. It took about three hours for the winds to subside. When the two rescue boats reached the canoe, they saw eight men holding on to it, though shivering due to the cold wind. They were helped into the rescue boats; it was noticed that the man who was missing was Homiah, who would still be under the capsized canoe. Horrified, the men turned it over. And there was my Homiah, all tangled up in the net. He was barely alive when they freed him and laid him in one of the rescue boats. They tried to resuscitate him but it was too late. When the boat arrived ashore with Homiah's body, it was met with wailing and dirges. I had already fainted from hearing the news that my beloved Homiah was the only casualty.

They brought Homiah's body to his father's compound and started the process for burial the next day. I was lost, scared, and in denial. "Homiah couldn't be gone. No, he couldn't be. There must be a mistake." It wasn't until his coffin was on the way to the cemetery that I came to accept that he was really truly gone for good.

As expected, although everyone could see what had led to Homiah's demise, his family wanted to know who or what force was behind it spiritually. People always believed that nobody died of natural causes. Every death had to be investigated for a spiritual cause. His older sister and two of his father's siblings took one of his garments to Komenle Awia, a prominent diviner and herbalist in Sanvoma. Komenle Awia was to Sanvoma what Priestess Yaba was to Aakonu. After several minutes of divination, he came out with his verdict: two men in the village had been jealous of Homiah's good fortune; they had therefore given him to the powerful god Anvola. Those who claim to see him spiritually say Anvola usually manifested himself as half fire and half human. So fearsome was he that the very thought of being given to him would send a person into depression.

It was this god who had caused the sudden storm to get to Homiah. He had so immobilized the great swimmer that he could not get out of the canoe in time like the others. Homiah's young relatives went straight to the home of the two men (Egya Nwole and his nephew Anwobo), whom Komenle Awia had named as the culprits. Like everyone else in Sanvoma these two were themselves in shock after hearing of Homiah's death. The two sides almost exchanged blows, but for the timely intervention of other villagers who took the men to the palace of Nana Nvuma, the chief of Sanvoma. Nana Nvuma and his elders advised Homiah's relatives to calm down. They understood their pain, but this wasn't the way to approach the issue. They should concentrate on giving their loved one a fitting burial. Afterwards, any question regarding the cause of death could be discussed. As the saying goes, "We do not stand in ants to remove ants." This was too fresh and too shocking for everybody. Moreover, it was doubtful if these two were really behind Homiah's death; a man so young and strong as he was would not go so quietly. In the minds of the elders, Homiah's ghost would likely show a sign that would help them confirm what was behind his death.

Ahu: Forever Changed

AT EIGHTEEN I WAS NOW a widow and had to go through the dreaded widowhood rites, though I was lucky to have been spared the part about keeping my husband's body company overnight. I did get my head shaved clean, which was the least I could do for this friend, husband and father of my children. I had always counted myself lucky with him. While my friends had to contend with multiple wives and elderly husbands, my Homiah had been just a few years older than me. Would he have married more wives later in life as Ebela's husband Amakyi had done? I will never know. All I know is that during my time with him, I was one of the most fortunate girls in Aakonu.

I was too shaken up to be fully aware of the funeral and burial arrangements. My mother and close family members took care of them and also looked after my two young children, Bomo and Noba. By the end of the day, my extended family as well as Homiah's had converged on the compound. The next morning my dear one lay in state in his father's compound in Sanvoma, and I sat by his side. Tears flowed freely as I pondered on our life together, how I would miss him, and what my life would be like now. People came from all over to console our families.

Homiah was buried that evening, though according to custom I could not go to the cemetery with him. Final funeral rites were held during the rest of the week, following which a "successor" was named. One of Homiah's uncles, the younger son of his maternal grandmother's sister, a medium-built, middle-aged man named Gokeh, was named his main successor, assisted by two distant cousins. Gokeh had lived in Obuasi where he was a goldsmith, but moved back to Sanvoma when his father was too old to take care of his coconut plantation. He already had two wives and five children of his own when he was named Homiah's successor.

Succession is a major custom among the Nzema people. A successor must undertake to take care of the responsibilities left behind by the deceased. Soon came the big question that always fell on a young widow. My husband's successor Gokeh had expressed interest in marrying me. With no inheritance, I had very limited means of caring for our two young children and the little one who was on the way. The small farm I cultivated was on land belonging to Homiah, and it would likely be taken over by Gokeh. The idea of a person leaving behind a will was alien to us. Even in the rare case where there was a will, many families neither understood nor saw the need for it.

There was the case of a distant relative who, because he had lived in the Bay Coast, one of the big, modern cities in the country, had made a will and in blatant deviation from custom left everything he had to his wife and children and nothing to his "family"—his parents, especially his mother, his sisters and their children. In our very matrilineal society, a man was said to belong to his mother's clan, while his children belonged to his wife's clan. This meant that in the eyes of his clan, his mother, brothers, sisters and his sisters' children were his real family. Even his mother's brothers, her sisters and their children were considered more family than his own wife and children. Thus the man was expected to make provision for his clan family in his will; leaving them out would be like "removing his intestines from his belly and filling it with leaves."

At his funeral his clan family would have none of this, accusing his wife of using witchcraft to turn the head of their kinsman and killing him so she could inherit his wealth. There was great commotion at the family home in Sanvoma where the body had been brought for burial. The man's successor, a nephew, tore up the will, and the funeral ceremonies were never completed, the clan family refusing to have the final sit-down after the burial. This meant they could not set a date for his annual anniversary during which they would have formally accounted for and shared all his property. The traumatized wife and children left for the city and never returned.

In my case, whether my children and I got the land, or anything else for that matter, would depend on the benevolence of Gokeh and whether I agreed to marry him or not. If I refused, I would have to leave my husband's compound and return to my family home in Aakonu with my children. I knew very well that taking care of them would be difficult. I was not looking for new suitors, and in any case few men would want to marry a widow with kids. Marrying Gokeh seemed the only logical option. I would be the third wife. It was hard at first for me to transition from the life I had with Homiah to a new life with Gokeh, from being an only wife of the man I loved to the third wife of someone much older and whom I barely knew. Fortunately I did not have to leave my husband's compound immediately to join Gokeh; I stayed in my home for a year until the anniversary of Homiah's passing. The first anniversary was when the deceased's material possessions were accounted for and shared among his relatives. Gokeh took whatever he fancied and gave the rest to his clan family members. The land was deemed family property, since Homiah had not cultivated any cash crop on it. This meant that I could continue to harvest cassava on the land for as long as I stayed married to Gokeh, and was willing and able to farm it, but I could not claim ownership of the land, or plant any cash crop or build on it.

It was during this time that I gave birth to our third child, Kane. I busied myself with the new baby, while my mother helped take care of the older children. I would have preferred to stop with the three children from Homiah; however, as I had no way of stopping myself from getting pregnant, I soon found myself pregnant again. This was two years after Homiah's passing. I was still living in Homiah's house where Gokeh came to visit occasionally. His own compound, where he lived with his first two wives, was a few compounds away from where I lived with my children.

It turned out to be a very difficult pregnancy. Morning sickness lasted till my second trimester. Into my twelfth week, I found that I was bleeding. Gokeh took me to a missionary clinic that had recently opened in Bokabo, a village ten kilometres away. I was told that I needed to rest. Unlike Priestess Yaba of Aakonu or Komenle Awia of Sonwoma, who would have explained which person was "behind" my problem, the nurses at the clinic gave me medicine that was foreign and rather bitter. Even though I stopped bleeding and felt better, my mother and I still went to see Priestess Yaba to find out who was behind the problem and what we needed to do to pacify any god I might have been given to or to nullify any evil spells. True to expectation, the priestess had a reason for my near-miscarriage. According to her, Homiah's spirit had been held hostage by the god who had killed him. He had been expecting a sacrifice before releasing him. However, since nobody had made the required sacrifice, he felt it was better to take my unborn child. If after taking the unborn child still nothing happened, then he would come for me.

"Yes, you heard right. You!" she hissed.

To avoid the calamity, my mother and I reported what we had been told to Gokeh and to Homiah's family. Fortunately, the family was responsive and gave the necessary sacrifice.

Initially, I attributed the saving of my pregnancy to that sacrifice rather than to the medication from the clinic. Some weeks later, however, I was stricken by malaria. Although it is a serious illness, many in the village treated it casually, like the common cold. They resorted to natural remedies that sometimes worked and sometimes didn't. My sickness started with the usual symptoms of fever, fatigue, and loss of appetite. When it wouldn't go away with some of the common remedies, I went to the bush and gathered some herbs, which I boiled when I got home. Then I sat on a stool, put the pot with the boiled herbs in it, covered myself with a thick blanket and opened the pot so that the steam from the pot engulfed my entire body. This process was used to help the body sweat out the sickness. It was my final recourse. In the evening I did the procedure again with more herbal medicines. After three days I felt better and went about my duties as usual. I was about seven months pregnant. And then one evening I began to feel sick again. I was shivering, and my head was hurting so badly that I felt it was going to explode. I had moved to my mother's compound in Aakonu earlier in the month to be under her care. She saw my condition and sent an emissary to inform my husband. She also called on the priestess, who came up with her own explanation and prescribed more sacrifices. The next day, when Gokeh came to see me, he said I should be sent to the clinic.

There were no cars or buses. He and three other men created an *ahomanga*—a long wooden pole of about eight feet, to which was attached a twelve-yard cotton cloth tied at both ends, making a cradle. They put me inside the cradle and with one person holding the front, another the middle, and a third one the rear, we set off on the ten-kilometre journey to the clinic in Bokabo. I tried to cope with the extreme discomfort and pain of the journey by recalling the good times I had had with Homiah. I recalled the day he came home from fishing, too hungry to wait for dinner to be ready. He cut up and rinsed the octopus and crabs he had brought, ground the tomatoes, peppers, and onions, mixed them all together with a bit of water and a pinch of salt and put it on the fire to cook for ten minutes. He got some akyeke, made from cassava, from Madam Adoma's makeshift market not too far from our compound. Madam Adoma's akyeke was one of the best in Sanvoma. Dinner was ready in less than twenty minutes. I left whatever I was cooking and joined him. It turned out to be the best meal we ever had. From then on he wouldn't stop teasing me about my cooking, how I took so much time and care but could never get it to taste like his hastily made entree. Looking back to those times made me realize how happy I had been.

A jolt of my makeshift carriage brought me back rudely from my daydream. The man in front had hit his leg on something and stumbled, almost causing the other two to fall over each other and drop their precious cargo. I screamed in pain, making them even more flustered. They put me down by the side of the road for a few minutes while they rested their shoulders and rotated their positions, the third man going to the front. An hour after we started, they got me to the clinic. It was a busy day as usual, but since my case was an emergency, they took me straight to what could be called the ER section. I was quickly checked in, admitted, and given infusions. It turned out that I was dehydrated. Gokeh thanked the helpers profusely and returned with them to the village, leaving my mother to stay with me to attend to my needs. After three days at the clinic I was better. I was given medication and advised about proper nutrition to ensure that my growing baby and I stayed healthy and well nourished. After I was discharged, I began to wonder what it was that made the people in the clinic so capable. Unlike the priestess, they did not talk about offering sacrifices to gods, though I was still a bit disappointed that they did not tell me who was behind my sickness. I found it difficult to accept that my sickness was caused by mosquitoes, and I needed to eat more greens. That was going to be really difficult. To me, greens were meant for farm animals, not humans. I did sometimes have soups and stews made with cocoyam leaves and red oil, which I loved. But there was no way I would be able to eat those cocoyam leaves if they were not cooked.

Once back in Aakonu I stayed healthy for the remaining months of my pregnancy. Other than the usual heaviness and discomfort due to my very large belly, I felt really good. On the day I went into labour, I woke up early as usual and was sweeping the compound when I started feeling the pain. After giving three births I was what one might call "experienced." I knew the signs. First the "show," then the ever intensifying back pain, then more pain from the contractions, the water breaks and within a few hours baby is here. My third baby Kane had virtually "just showed up." This time I felt the contractions intensify, but because I was expecting the show, I did not think it was labour. By the time I realized and called out for the elderly woman who was attending to me, the baby was already on her way. But it seemed that baby number four was in no hurry to come out. At around two AM the next day the pain had become unbearable. Nana checked me and was unwilling to call Bozoma, the elderly traditional birth attendant at that hour. By four AM, when she realized I needed urgent help, she had no choice but to go and bring her. Madam Bozoma checked me and did what she needed to do. I was still in great pain. At around ten in the morning, when it felt like the baby was coming, they carried me to the multipurpose bathroom of the compound to deliver. Madam Bozoma called her assistant, Enoku to help her. After about five more hours of pain and no sign of the baby, it was time to do something else. Memories of my biological mother, Mame Azira, who died in childbirth twenty-four years ago was by now tagging at everyone's mind.

But soon both Madam Bozoma and Enoku realized what was going on—this baby was coming out legs first, which was not a good sign. In most such cases the mother almost always ended up dying. Only an evil child would do such a thing as come out leg first. Really! Either the baby had been bewitched as a way to get at the mother, or the baby was itself paying for an evil deed done in another life.

"Why me, why this baby? Who is behind this? Could Homiah still be behind this? No, not the Homiah I knew. He would not do such a thing, and especially not to me."

Nana was still at Priestess Yaba's compound when my husband Gokeh, whom my attendants had called, now that my situation was getting out of hand, advised that I should be sent back to the clinic in Bokabo once again. Madam Bozoma sent Enoku to go and get Nana while I was helped into the makeshift carrier.

Nana had arrived and reported to Gokeh what the Priestess had said. Gokeh had no time for it. He told Nana to forget about that and focus on getting me to the clinic. Reluctantly, Nana packed a few items and soon we were on our way to Bokabo. We got there around five PM. By now the clinic staff knew me by name. They immediately checked me out and prepared me for a caesarean section. When they were told I was to be operated on, my family members started wailing. As far as Nana was concerned I might as well be dead. She blamed herself for not applying the perfumed water on me first like the Priestess had advised rather than follow Gokeh's advise to come to the clinic. In Aakonu people usually avoided the clinic for fear of being operated upon. The next few hours felt like eternity. Nana and Gokeh were not allowed inside, so they stayed in the waiting area, eagerly looking at every staff member who passed by for some information. They had braced themselves for the unthinkable. In about two hours one of the nurses emerged to call them to the doctor's office. Dr Ama Boah, a middle-aged friendly woman with glasses, welcomed them. She told them the operation had been successful and I had delivered a bouncy baby girl. They were ecstatic.

I was discharged in two weeks. It was a special homecoming for me and my baby. So excited was I that I bucked tradition and named my daughter Menyena ("I didn't expect it"). From then on I had a different perception altogether of the clinic. I was especially grateful, knowing that if my family had not taken me there, I would not have made it.

I remembered Ebela's case very well, and that made me even more sure of how fortunate I had been. I resolved that at least one of my children would do whatever it was that Dr Ama Boah and her nurses, who saved my life and that of Menyena, did.

Ahu: A New Beginning

THERE WAS AN ELEMENTARY SCHOOL in Aakonu, owned and run by the Catholic Church. The small church building was made of cement blocks and stood out at the north end of the main street, one of only two buildings made of cement blocks. The other was the chief's palace. The church was roofed with bright corrugated iron sheets that shone in the sun. It had started as an outpost of the main church at Bokabo and had been established with the clinic seven years earlier. A priest from Bokabo came over once every three months to hold mass. Other Sundays a local man named Egya Nze led the service.

We had an interesting relationship with the church. To many of us the church was just another meeting place. A few people went to service every Sunday; those same people would be at Priestess Yaba's compound if they had any ailment. Some people did get baptized and were given Christian names like Mary, Elizabeth, Joseph, and John. These were considered as just additions to the names they already had. Outside of the church or the school, nobody remembered those names. In many ways, the church's teaching of one man one wife and belief in only one god did not align with the way of life of the people, hence the low level of interest among the opinion leaders in the village.

Next to the church was the elementary school. It consisted of a long hut made of raffia sticks and roofed with thatch. It was divided into four rooms, three of which served as classrooms and the other an office. Only a few children attended the school, mostly boys, though most of them, like Kakukyi, Mozu, and Ndabia, left by the time they were old enough to start working with their fathers in the various fishing groups. I had decided that I would enroll all my children in the school, and my eldest, Bomo, was already attending when Menyena was born. I had also already decided not to have any more children, given how close I had come to losing my life giving her birth. As I expected, my husband strongly disagreed. As far as he was concerned, it was not my decision to make. As long as I had not reached menopause, the only way I could stop having children would be to stop sleeping with my husband. But how would he justify being married to me if he could not sleep with me? Gokeh was clear that as long as I stayed under his roof in Sanvoma, he would not tolerate my decision not to have more children.

I decided therefore to continue to stay with Nana at Opanin Nda's compound in Aakonu rather than return to my marital home, even after Menyena was six months old and I had no reason to continue staying with Nana. I figured that staying there would give my body enough time to heal and also keep me from getting pregnant again. The concept of artificial birth control was unheard of. Eventually my husband decided that it wasn't worth his while to be married only in name to a woman who would rather be with her mother. He decided to divorce me and move on with his life.

If Gokeh saw the divorce as punishment, I saw it as liberating.

I used my new-found freedom to focus on caring for my children. I opened a small eatery in the village, the kind locally known as "chop bar," where I served breakfast and lunch with the help of Nana and my older children Bomo and Noba. My rice and fufu with palm nut soup, light soup, or peanut butter soup became the talk of the village. Everyday, except Tuesday and Sunday, when the fishermen did not go to sea, I would leave the eatery in the care of Nana and go to the beach to buy fish for the following day's cooking. The younger fishermen would troop to my eatery for their lunch or dinner once they came back from work. Within three years I had transformed myself from a sad, recently widowed third wife who relied on her husband for her survival to a self-assured woman who knew what she wanted for her children and would do everything she could to get it. This, of course, did not come without consequences. In our close-knit society where women and girls were expected to know their place and stay in it, my nonconforming attitude earned disapproval. Husbands did not want their wives to become friends with me, for fear that I would infect them with my "witchcraft." At the annual Kundum festival, the men sang songs mocking me. I was becoming a danger, they sang, warning husbands to shield their wives from my influence.

Kundum is celebrated to acknowledge a year of abundance, expel evil, and thank the gods. Legend has it that a hunter, known only as Akpoley, came upon a group of dwarfs drumming and dancing the Kundum dance while he was out hunting. He hid himself and studied the dance. When he returned home he taught it to the people in his village called Aboade, who loved it so much that they embraced it as their own festival. The Kundum festival started at Aboade and made its way westward to the other villages along the coast over the weeks that followed. The Kundum god was believed to be paralyzed on one half of his body, and so he moved slowly from one village to the next. The festival reached Aakonu around mid-October. The people used the preceding week to cleanse themselves, perfect their dances, maintain the drums, and practice the songs they would sing. These songs were narratives. When the festival started the people welcomed it outside the village, then proceeded to the main market square where the drums were brought. For that entire week, the period between two in the afternoon to the small hours of the morning was devoted to Kundum dancing and general merrymaking. From the third day onwards the chief, Nana Ngoma II and the queen mother, Obahemaa Ekeleba would be carried in palanquins to the festival grounds. The chief's wife and children, unfortunately, had no critical role to play in the royal house since they were considered to be from a different family from their husband and father, the chief.

When the chief and his elders were seated, a group of youths would arrive, holding on to a long horizontal pole, dressed in special festival attire, with the ringing anklets tied round their legs making a lot of noise as they moved. They would narrate in proverbs every single thing that the chief and his council of elders had done that were disapproved of by the people. Embarrassing details would emerge from these narrations, such as about chiefs having sold land they had held in trust for the people or disputes they had unjustly resolved. It was not only the chief and his elders whose misdeeds were revealed this way. Stories emerged of men going after other men's wives, those who had stolen other people's property, and those who had lied or colluded with others to circumvent justice, people who had killed or sent others to be attacked by the gods. They even sang about Egya Amakyi after what happened to Ebela and her subsequent decision to leave him for the younger Mozu. Whatever the misdeed, they would sing about it. The expectation was that the wrong-doers would feel ashamed enough to acknowledge their wrongdoings and leave them with the Kundum god to carry away on his journey.

Egya Amakyi's case was not really a misdeed but an embarrassment best forgotten. The specific instances where people were accused of using spirits to cause the deaths of others were usually sad because, unlike physically verifiable crimes, there really was no way of knowing whether these accusations were true or not. So whatever was said usually stuck to the person. In my case there was nothing spiritual about it. People saw the change in me and felt I was not a good example for their wives to associate with. While I was surprised at how seriously people had taken my behaviour, I did not let that bother me too much.

Ahu: The People's River

RIVER AMANZULE AND THE VILLAGE of Aakonu have a special relationship. From its source at the lake near the famous Nzulezo (village on stilts), the river meanders along a narrow route almost one hundred kilometres long, bordered on both sides by thick green mangrove, and passes Aakonu on its way to the sea. Here it grows from a narrow stream into a wide river. It is a critical resource for the people of Aakonu. Its rich store of fish, shrimps, crabs, and other shellfish is a major source of livelihood for the people.

The first job of many children, before they were old enough to venture out to the sea with the grown-ups, was to collect periwinkle snail for sale. These tiny nutritious creatures were hard to find. They hid in the mud under the very tight mangrove roots. To the kids it was an adventure weaving through those tight mangroves at the edge of the river to pick them. That was one thing Bomo, my eldest daughter, was very good at. Her petite figure gave her added advantage over the other kids, who were tall and sturdy. On a good Saturday, after six hours of work, each child would bring home about twenty margarine tins full of periwinkle snails. At five shillings a tin this would bring in about four dollars. On weekdays the children would spend most of the day in school and so would not be able to work. For those who did, what they caught would become part of the family's evening meal.

After school, the children would find themselves fresh coconuts for lunch and head to the river to play before heading home. Ours was a community in the real sense of the word. At the riverside each person was everyone's responsibility. Those who were better swimmers took it upon themselves to help the younger and newer learners. Nobody paid any money and nobody expected to be paid for teaching others to swim. By their third visit to the river the learners would be swimming like fish.

The river had spiritual significance for the village. Not only was it seen as a protector, it was also worshipped as a deity, a male one. Once every year people sacrificed two large sheep (male and female) and countless chickens to him. They did not throw them into the river afterwards; they provided the people of Aakonu with a great lamb and chicken meal that was otherwise beyond their means. The meat was cooked and shared at a spot on the bank of the river where a small shrine had been built for the god, under a large neem tree. Whether it was the quiet chill under the huge tree or the presence of the god, one always felt a certain heaviness in the area. During the sacrifice, some portion of the meat was saved and given to the river god by his elderly spokesman, a man named Aka, who was said to have been chosen by the god to play this role at age thirteen. If you heard the god being described by the people, you would think Egya Aka was his human twin. He was a tall, handsome man with beautiful black skin and a stern demeanor. As he burnt the sacrifice, he led the people to give thanks and seek the protection of the river god for the year ahead.

I recall a day in June when the entire landscape of Aakonu changed forever. June is the climax of the rainy season in the area. The river had already overflowed its banks. The sea had also risen substantially. However, during my lifetime and even from what I have been told, the sea and the river had always stayed within their boundaries. What happened that day in June became the talk of the village for a long time. As was our custom, my friends Ndabela and Manye and I went to sleep at the beach after a wonderful time playing *anyima*. The weather was a bit gloomy but it did not look like there would be rain anytime soon. It was one of those days when the sun was playing hide-and-seek. Usually when that happened it didn't rain. Therefore why not enjoy a good sleep in the breeze rather than be stuck indoors?

Most families slept under mosquito nets. However, nets were restrictive. When it was very warm, you would wake up drenched in sweat. In some homes you would have four children on a bed. On an open raffia bed the children could roll around without any problem, but when they were squished together under a net it became a different story altogether. Some kids went all crazy at night, and if you found yourself under the same net, it became truly intolerable. To get away from my siblings and enjoy the breeze, I slept on the beach with my friends at every opportunity.

That day I joined them after I had completed my chores, and we proceeded together to the beach. We each put down our piece of cloth and lay side by side. There was a beautiful breeze blowing and soon we were sound asleep. At around midnight the rains started. My friends and I ran home as fast as we could, under fierce thunder and lightning. In the absence of drains the entire village of Aakonu became one large gulley. The water was running down so fast we had to hold on to the poles and raffia walls of houses to keep from being swept away. Before long the sea had risen beyond its boundary and was approaching the village square. The raffia houses were no match for its anger. Before long those that were close to the beach were being carried away; people ran out in a panic, taking with them whatever they could. At the same time the river to the east and the small streams to the north were all overflowing. There was nowhere for us to go. We huddled on the small strip of land yet uncovered by the waters. It was a nightmare.

By the morning the rain had finally subsided, but the damage would take a long time to be fixed. As expected, the Priestess Yaba, whose compound seemed miraculously untouched, and Egya Aka, spokesman for the Amanzule River, had an explanation: the river god was angry. He had teamed up with the sea to cause the havoc we had just experienced. Now what? What if he asked for a higher sacrifice than the usual sheep and chicken?

Fearful of the flood recurring and they would not be as lucky, many people relocated inland, about five kilometres away from Aakonu and the sea, where they rebuilt their homes. The new place was called Aakonu Fofole (New Aakonu). For others it would take more than a single weather phenomenon or anger from the river god to move from their dear village to anywhere else, even if that new place was safer and only a few kilometres away. For those of us who stayed, however, the altered landscape meant a permanent change in our sleeping arrangements. Although the raised sandy bank that served as the sea's boundary was still intact, albeit a lot flatter than it used to be, the people were a lot more cautious now and slept with one eye open for the next big wave.

In the east the river had created a second route to Aakonu—a new, five-hundred-metre long tributary that stopped at the edge of the village. The hitherto long strip of land between the village and the river was now a very narrow strip, and an even smaller barrier between it and the sea. My family were among those who stayed. I would not give up my village for any place else. My only regret, as I would later tell my grandchildren, was that there were no cameras for us to record and share pictures of our village as it was before the unexpected visitor came to town.

Bomo: School

I ENROLLED MY CHILDREN BOMO, Noba, Kane, and Menyena in the local school as soon as they became eligible. Bomo was the first and as eager as anything. When she was younger, I never failed to let her know how important education was. I told her what Dr Ama Boah and her team at the clinic in Bokabo had done to virtually pluck me from the jaws of death. Even today, the clinic, now a hospital, continues to be the main provider of primary health care to the people. Even with the little resources at their disposal, they continue to provide quality healthcare to thousands every month, from day to day illnesses like malaria, typhoid, dysentery and others, to performing risky deliveries and surgeries, and advising patients battling chronic diseases like diabetes, high blood pressure, and cancers.

I would tell her, "Bomo, if it wasn't for that doctor and her people, neither I nor your sister Menyena would be alive today. I know I am too old to do this. That is why I want you and your siblings to take school seriously and become like her. I want you to become somebody else's testimony someday."

Bomo knew from my tone that what I said was very important.

I remember her holding on to my cloth when we arrived at the school the first day. She was six years old. School was in session when we got there. Children had just finished the morning assembly and were marching into their classrooms. One elderly teacher directed them to their classrooms while the two middle aged men carried inside drums that were used at the assembly. There was no dedicated assembly hall, and so morning assembly and other gatherings took place in the open. Once the students were inside, the elderly man met me in the one room that served as the office. He already knew what I was there for. After all, how often does a mother show up at the school with a six-year-old in tow, if not to be enrolled in school? The elderly man, known by most of us as *Kyekya* (Teacher) Joseph (he was the only one who was known by his church name), whom I later got to know as the head teacher and responsible for the younger children, asked Bomo to put her hand over her head and touch her other ear with it. If she was able to do it, that meant she was ready for school. I had put a clean dress on her. She wore no sandals; few children in Aakonu wore them. Those who did, wore them only when they went on a journey. I waited while Kyekya Joseph wrote down her name. He gave her a slate and a piece of chalk and asked her to join the other children, who were seated on the floor in the classroom for six- and seven-year-olds, ie Classes One and Two pupils. There were about twelve children in that class. The other two classrooms were for Classes Three and Four and Classes Five and Six respectively. There were two more teachers in addition to the headteacher, and about thirty-two children in all. Once the children finished Class Six, they could continue their schooling in the nearby villages of Kamunu and Bokabo. Most children dropped out at that point, the boys to join their fathers and older brothers in the fishing business.

The long hut that served as the school had four rooms which served as three classrooms and an office. Each classroom had two doors, one on each side. The walls were made entirely of raffia sticks, held together on each side by wooden beams into which the raffia sticks were nailed. The roof was thatch. A long, wooden upright pole supported the roof in the middle, and one on each end of the structure.

The raffia wall on each side reached up to two-thirds of the full height of the hut and allowed for ventilation. There were no compounds between the school and the beach. This meant that the breezes blew in from the beach, and the kids could also hear the waves and sometimes also, when the fishing canoes returned ashore, the raucous sounds of the fishermen and their customers. There were four moringa trees outside, at vantage points that provided shade and served as a place for the children to congregate when not in their classrooms.

There were two school sessions. The morning session ran from 8 to 11.30 AM. The children would go home for lunch and return at 12.30 and stay till closing time at 3.30. By the third day, Bomo couldn't wait to go to school. She enjoyed writing on her slate with her chalk and was intrigued by the stories Kyekya Joseph told them. Every day was a whole new adventure.

By the time she was in Class Four, Bomo was ahead of the other children. She loved all the subjects, especially arithmetic, reading, and science. Although naturally shy, she seemed to be a different person when in school. When her brothers started school she couldn't wait to show them around. She would help them with their work at school, and at home she would sit them down after dinner to teach them.

A memorable incident from her elementary school experience happened in Class Four, when they began to write with pens.

Before then, they wrote with chalk in Class One and pencil in Classes Two and Three. Gokeh had bought her a beautiful pen. It was a "spring pen," the type you press to write with. Bomo was so enamored of it that she wouldn't put it down. One day an older boy in her class forced the pen out of her hand, causing the spring inside it to fall out into the sand. It couldn't be found. Bomo was incensed. She held on to the boy's shorts so tightly he couldn't wriggle himself out. She held onto him, all the while screaming at the top of her lungs, until the teacher came around and asked her to let him go.

Nothing made me happier than the fact that my children, especially my eldest daughter, had taken so well to school. I was determined to make sure they reached the highest level possible. I did not know at the time how I would be able to afford it if Bomo or any of her siblings were able to make it beyond the local school.

Although Bomo was doing well, I worried that the village school might not prepare her well enough. It didn't take a lot for anyone to see the disparity between the resources available to schools in the bigger towns and in the small villages, especially those that were far from the regional and district centres. Many teachers declined postings to these places, and so they were always short of teachers at the higher primary levels. Ours was one such village. Nestled between a river and the sea made it attractive to a water-loving person like me, but this meant that many teachers who could not swim or were afraid of rivers did not want to come anywhere near it.

And so I was delighted when I heard that one of Nana's cousins called Mieza was a teacher in a secondary school in Awiane, a much bigger town about one hundred kilometres northwest of Aakonu. I sent a message to him regarding Bomo and told him my wish for her to be able to attend a good school. He agreed that Bomo could come and stay with him. She would help around the house, cleaning and doing chores while also attending the elementary school nearby. When I told Bomo that she would be going to stay with this relative she felt both happy and sad. She was excited to be going to a place that was bigger than Aakonu and had a secondary school. But she was sad to be leaving me, her Nana, and her sister and brothers. They were growing up in their different ways and she loved being big sister. The day before she left, I made Bomo's favourite dish, rice and palm nut soup with beans, fresh fish, and periwinkle snail and gave her a double portion of that for her lunch. She spent the rest of the day washing her clothes, saying goodbye to her best friends Eduku, Akasi, and Akuba and playing with her siblings.

Uncle Mieza had come to get her and stayed overnight. This was Bomo's first time meeting him. He was a medium-built man of few words. Family gossip said that too much learning had affected his mind. He had unusually bushy hair for a man. That was one thing Bomo noticed. She thought that could be because the men in the bigger towns wore their hair like that. She helped me get him his food, and water to bathe once the initial akwaaba (welcome) was over.

She had so many questions to ask him, but she waited so as not to appear rude. She was eager to find out about the school, how many pupils there were, what the secondary school was like, how old the students were, what food they ate, whether he knew how to cook, and if so, who had taught him, and most importantly, whether she would be able to visit us once she had gone to stay with him. Nobody had mentioned earlier whether or not Uncle Mieza had a wife and children. If he did, she wondered what they did and would she get along with them? If he didn't, why not? She pondered these questions in her head until her uncle finished his bath and was ready to respond to her.

Awiane had both Catholic and Methodist elementary schools, he said. Bomo would attend the Methodist school since that was closer to where he lived, alone in one of the bungalows allocated to teachers of the secondary school where he taught English Literature. He got his food from the school, but occasionally did his own cooking. She would have her own room. Bomo was excited by that. At home in Aakonu, there was nothing like privacy. Her siblings came and went as they pleased. Even her mother did not have her own room. It was all five of them in one room, half of which served as the living room. At night they would roll down their mat and go to sleep. But this arrangement was not all bad. If she had a nightmare, her siblings and mother were there to console her. There were stories of gods and ghosts that made people sick, witches coming after children who made them angry, elders turning into snakes to bite disrespectful children. All these, plus the recent stories of the deaths of many children that had been attributed to witches spreading measles to kill and eat them. Now she would have her own room and no one to console her if she had a nightmare.

Bomo: First Lorry Ride

THE NEXT DAY NOBA, KANE, Menyena, Nana and I saw Bomo and Mieza off at the riverside. I put Bomo's clothes in a small jute bag, including my favourite two-yard cotton cloth that she could use to cover herself when going to sleep. Bomo was delighted to have it. She would have a piece of mother to comfort her when she slept. The one-hundred-kilometre journey to Awiane where uncle Mieza lived would take them the entire day. There were no good roads out of Aakonu. They did the first fifteen kilometres in a canoe down the river to get to Ayinam. From there they took one of the lorries that plied the road to take them to NewTown. That was Bomo's first ever ride in a lorry. There would be two more lorry rides before they reached Awiane.

In those days lorries ruled the roads. The driver's cabin in front had space for one passenger. Behind was the wooden body with wooden planks for seats. The average truck had about eight of these planks, each with space for ten passengers. When the truck was full, the extra passengers would hang on at the sides. There were no buses and even fewer private cars. Bomo was fascinated by the painted inscriptions on the backs and fronts of the lorries.

Their messages ranged from the inspirational to the spiteful—

"So it is"

"Eyes are watching"

"God will provide"

"Enemies are worried"

"Enemies are not God"

"And so what?"

"Nyamenle Kye a Benve," meaning, "When God shares something everyone gets their share."

The owners of these lorries were known to be wealthy. Their lorries were named after them, but they employed a relative or an acquaintance to drive them. The driver would have an apprentice, serving as mate, collecting fares and helping to load and offload passengers and their luggage. The driver's mate was usually not paid a wage but received a daily sum depending on how much the truck had earned on that day.

Not wanting to miss anything on this journey, Bomo stayed awake all day and all night. Not that she would have been comfortable if she had wanted to sleep. Every pothole, and there were many on the road, every swerve to avoid an oncoming lorry, jolted and swung the passengers left to right, making them collide with their neighbours. When the lorry braked, they would all be jolted forward and then backward. Bomo was too curious and excited to get scared. She was especially fascinated by the coconut trees that seemed to move past them one after another.

She and Uncle Mieza arrived at their destination early the next day. It was her very first time seeing tall buildings. It was as if somebody had put a ruler down and built them in straight line. Around them were green lawns rather than the sand she was used to in Aakonu. The school buildings and the student dormitories were neatly painted. Compared to the huts in her village they looked huge. Initially she wondered how the people on the upper floor balconies got there. It was later, when she had a chance to visit one that she saw that there were stairs that led to the upper floors.

Her uncle's unit was one of twenty staff quarters. It had three bedrooms, a study, a hall, a kitchen, one toilet and a bath. There were a storeroom and a lot of cupboards for storage. Bomo had never seen so many rooms in a home for one person. She thought she might lose her way here. When Uncle Mieza showed her her room she was lost for words. A room for herself, with a bed, a closet, and a study table with chair! There were fixtures on the ceiling that her uncle said used to light like lanterns, but they did not work anymore because there was no electricity. Instead, there were three lanterns in the house, one for the hall and one each for her and her uncle's bedrooms. If she had to be in the kitchen she would take her lantern with her. On the south side of her uncle's quarters was a soccer field where the students played among themselves or against other schools. Bomo was enamored with the students she saw. They were mostly teenagers who lived in the boarding house on campus and virtually ran their own affairs. Led by the prefects who were elected from among the junior year class at the end of every academic year, the student body managed their life on campus, from looking after the grounds, going to their evening classes, and keeping general discipline. There were housemasters and housemistresses who complemented the student leadership, gave guidance, and served as judges in situations which the students could not handle themselves.

By the Monday following her arrival, she was ready for school. Unlike the pupils in her school in Aakonu, the children here all wore clean, well-ironed uniforms, shoes, and socks. The first few weeks went by and she made friends with the other students in the staff quarters. Her favourite pastime was to chase the birds as they flew in flocks to feed on the grass in front of her uncle's house. In Aakonu the only birds she saw were seagulls, which chased after the fish that escaped out of the fishing nets as they were being pulled ashore by the fishermen, and vultures that fed on leftover fish and other dead animals. These birds were different. They were easy to follow as they hopped about without flying away. Bomo felt they were playing catch with her.

One event would always stick in her mind. It was Saturday morning. She had finished her chores and was playing outside with the birds when she saw something that looked like a bird stuck in the electrical lines on the poles in front of her house. It did not move when she tried to get its attention. She realized that it could be dead, so she went inside to inform Uncle Mieza about it. Using a long stick they were able to get it to the ground. It turned out to be a large bat. They started throwing ideas about what to do with it. Neither Bomo nor Uncle Mieza had eaten bat meat before. Her uncle related to her the biblical story of the Israelites being provided with quail for their meal.

Uncle Mieza knew the Bible from beginning to end. In fact, every possible frame on every door in the house was covered in biblical verses. That morning happened to be the one when he had said that he had no money for food. When school was in session he would be served food from the dining hall. One of the students was in charge of taking his plates to the dining hall and bringing it back with food. During the vacation they had to cook their own meals. It was no coincidence that he saw the dead bat as providential meat for the day.

Bomo did not know how to prepare a bat, though she had

assisted her mother when she cooked chicken for special family dinners. All girls were expected to know how to cook, and she did not want to disappoint her uncle, so she went ahead with preparing a bat soup. She took the bat, cleaned and cut it up. They did not have any of the ingredients she needed to make the soup, so she asked her uncle for money to go to the market.

The market was about five kilometres away. She knew that although the items she needed were sold close to where she lived, they were too expensive compared to the main market. On her way, Bomo heard that there had been a big catch of fish that day. The fish market was not too far from where she was going so she decided to check out the bumper catch and if possible buy some fish. She was not disappointed. There was more fish here than she had ever seen in her life. Unlike the canoes in her village, the fishing boats here were large and powered by outboard motors. She was surprised at the sheer number of such boats carrying loads of various types of fish. She used half of her money to buy fish, very pleased with herself for what she thought was a great bargain. She proceeded to the main market and bought the ingredients she needed for her soup. Because she had spent half of her cash on fish, she could buy only small portions of the soup ingredients.

She reached home after three hours, and with great excitement went in search of Uncle Mieza to share her good news. To her surprise, Uncle Mieza was livid. Why was she so late? Why did she buy fish when she had not been asked to? What did she intend to do with the fish? Bomo did not know what to say. She had not expected such a reaction. Her uncle withdrew to his room for what seemed forever, but he returned to the kitchen finally.

"Bomo," he called her in a stern voice.

"Yes, Uncle," she responded.

"Here is what the Lord says. Since you went out of your way to get fish when you had not been asked to, you will have to eat the fish until it is finished. This also means that you will not have any of the bat soup that you will be preparing."

While she was relieved that she wouldn't suffer any real punishment for her "waywardness," she was sad that she did not get to taste the bat soup. The rest of the week she ate steamed fish, fish soup, fish stew, fried fish, and smoked fish.

It did not take long before Bomo noticed that things were not going too well with her uncle. School had been back in session for about three weeks. The young student, Nicholas, who was in charge of getting her uncle's food from the dining hall had been coming as expected. One day, at the start of the fourth week Bomo noticed that there was nothing for breakfast, because when Nicholas came to get their bowls, Uncle Mieza had failed to open the door. Once when Bomo heard the young man knocking and ran towards the door, her uncle stopped her. He said the Lord had not said she could open the door. Bomo watched the young man go away after standing around for about fifteen minutes without a response. She assumed that if her uncle had refused to let the young man bring their breakfast, then he would have some other plan for their breakfast. But this was not so. The Lord had not given the go-ahead, which meant that she had to go to school hungry. She did not know what to do. That day in school was the longest she had ever endured. By the third period she was too hungry to concentrate. She could not remember a day when she and her siblings had gone hungry at home.

Back home in Aakonu she would finish her chores, take her bath, and get herself ready for school. By the time she was done there would be a bowl of rice and palm nut soup with beans waiting for her. Sometimes, if she was running late, Nana would pour her food into a large clean leaf and fold the sides to seal it inside.

Bomo relished eating her breakfast from the leaf as she ran to school. She would be done eating by the time she got to school.

She was relieved when school was finally over, and she went home expecting that the Lord had given her uncle permission to let Nicholas get their food. Unfortunately, by the time she got home he had already come and gone without being able to bring lunch. Bomo was devastated. How was she expected to live on an empty stomach? Uncle Mieza was hunched over his Bible. When she first arrived at Uncle Mieza's house from Aakonu and saw Bible verses written with chalk on every doorpost in the house, she did not think much of it. Now it all seemed to fit together. Uncle Mieza's god seemed to dictate how even mundane things like meals happened in this house. The bat soup episode was still fresh on her mind. This was not what she had signed up for, she thought to herself.

When Bomo could not bear her hunger any longer, she started to cry. She thought of what they would be having for dinner in her mother's home. Her uncle saw her crying and brought her three unripe mangoes in a bowl of water to eat. The sight of them made Bomo cry even more. She cried herself to sleep without touching the mangoes.

The next day she went to school without expecting anything for breakfast. Fearing that there would be nothing to eat at home, Bomo followed one of her new school friends, Abenlema, home for lunch. Abenlema lived with her parents in a big, two-storey house close to the main lorry station and about two kilometres from Uncle Mieza's house. Abenlema and Bomo were opposites. Abenlema was tall for her age while Bomo was petite. Abenlema was a jovial, life-of-the-party kind of girl while Bomo was shy and preferred reading by herself to playing games or engaging in idle chat. Abenlema was the first girl to approach the shy Bomo when she first showed up in their class. She introduced her to her friends. She had a lot of friends because of her outgoing nature, and also because she brought a lot of goodies like candy and biscuits to school. It was no wonder that Bomo confided in her about what was happening at her home.

At Abenlema's home Bomo ate so much that for a moment it reminded her of her home in Aakonu. She missed her home even more. The feeling of family and the abundance of food at Abenlema's house made her realize how cold and isolated she was in Uncle Mieza's house.

She had no way of sending a message to her mother that she was starving, and how much she missed them. Finally, after three days of missing food at Uncle Mieza's, she made up her mind. She would not sit around and starve. She would find her way back home to Aakonu. All she needed to do was get to NewTown, the main market town where most of the women from her village came to trade. If she got there on a market day, she was sure to find someone to go home with.

She packed her few items into a paper bag and hid it under her bed. Friday morning came. It was a market day, and she waited until her uncle had gone to teach his class. Wearing her school uniform so as to appear she was going to school late, she made her way to the lorry station and found one to drop her at the market town. She had borrowed from Abenlema, to which she added the small amount of pocket money her mother had given her, to pay her fare.

This time the journey did not seem as long. She was as excited as she was hungry. Now her only concern was to get to NewTown in time to meet women from Aakonu. Since neither her mother nor Uncle Mieza knew where she was, if anything happened to her no one would know. Fortunately she got to the town in time, at eleven PM, moments before the next lorry left. How relieved she was to meet Ndabela, her mother's very good friend, in the lorry. They reached Bokabo at two a.m. It was too late to proceed, so Ndabela took her to the home of an acquaintance of hers where they spent the rest of the night. Early the next morning they continued their journey on foot and arrived at the riverside, where they got on a canoe to take them down to Aakonu. Getting off the canoe, she walked the five hundred metres to her home.

Bomo was filled with a myriad emotions. And the family were happy to see her. At the same time Nana and I had a lot of questions. Where was Uncle Mieza? Why did he leave Bomo to undertake the journey by herself? We were angry at Mieza when we heard Bomo's story. Nana decided that she would send an emissary to inform him about Bomo's safe arrival, and use the opportunity to tell him what Bomo had recounted. We wanted his version. As the elders would say, *we do not roof only one half of a house.* We would wait to hear Mieza's version of events before deciding on the right course of action to take.

It was six months before Mieza visited Aakonu. By then Bomo had already forgotten about her ordeal. She was happy to be back home with her brothers and sister, her Nana, and me, her mother. She did not have to worry about going to bed hungry. She did notice Nana whisper some very tough words to Uncle Mieza the day after he arrived. Uncle Mieza tried to explain but the older woman was firm. This was no way to treat a child. Bomo walked stealthily out of the room before they could find out she was there. Uncle Mieza returned to his station the next day. Bomo was glad she did not have to see him off this time.

Bomo: Egya Amakyi's Coconuts

BOMO FINALLY COMPLETED PRIMARY SCHOOL in Aakonu, which only went up to Class Six. This meant that for middle school she had to go somewhere else. I decided to enroll her at the middle school in Kamunu. Not only was it closer than others, it was also a better resourced school than other schools in the vicinity. People said it got some additional funding from outside the district due to its special status as an Islamic school. Moreover, many people from Aakonu frequented there to sell fish, so the footpath that led to the place was fairly well travelled and hence safer. I had sold fish in this village when I was growing up, and so I knew quite a few people well enough to be comfortable to let Bomo attend school there. The only problem was that Kamunu is located to the south west of Aakonu, which meant that Bomo and her fellow classmates had to cross River Amanzule every day to be able to go to school and back.

Every morning she and twelve other children would cross the river in the community canoe and make the rest of the journey to Kamunu on foot, five kilometres away. The teachers did not care that Bomo and her colleagues from Aakonu crossed a river to get to school. Latecomers were either caned or made to weed plots of land as punishment. Bomo was so scared in the beginning that she hardly slept for fear of oversleeping and getting to school late. While her primary school was a Catholic school, the middle school happened to be an Islamic school. This did not matter much. Every morning the pupils assembled in rows in front of the school and facing east, recited the Islamic prayer. Then the morning announcements were made, following which the teacher on duty would go around with a big cane, inspecting uniforms, nails, teeth, and general cleanliness. Anyone failing this inspection or not paying attention could end up saying hello to the cane as the teachers used to say. Bomo did not let down her guard. School was her ticket to a better life for herself, her family, and possibly her whole community, and so she had to stay focused. But it was not all just boring arithmetic and reading.

There were a few things that she would remember fondly about her time in middle school. There was this crush of hers when she was in Form Two. To Bomo, Nyameke was the most handsome boy she had ever met. He was athletic, of medium built, and very smart. He wore his hair in a box cut that laid out his boyish, innocent-looking face. Bomo was lively and happy whenever he was in class, and when he was absent she found herself looking out the window expectantly. She felt especially good when she beat him in the periodic class quizzes. When they interacted, they would argue about one thing or another, and she would pretend that she really did not care much about him. Only she knew how much she was crushing on him.

Bomo and her classmates from Aakonu were good friends with their Muslim classmates. However, there could be nothing more than friendships, since Muslims could not date non-Muslims. If a non-Muslim boy or girl wanted to date or marry a Muslim, they were required to become Muslim. Of course, none of their parents would hear of such a thing, and so it stayed an unwritten rule that they went to school, had friends at school, and studied. The Muslim festivals of Eid Al-Fitr and Eid Al-Adha were a lot of fun. On the main days of these celebrations, food was in abundance. They would eat lots of lamb and chicken soup with rice, and fufu. There were games and other activities to engage in as well. It was a good thing to look forward to. What she did not like was the month of fasting that preceded the Eid Al-Fitr holiday. During that month none of the Muslim students ate between sunrise and sunset. It also meant that nobody sold any food or snacks in school. Bomo and her friends had to make sure they brought food from home, else they would have to go the entire school day without eating until they got to the coconut trees on their way home from school.

They had a lot of fun going to and from school. At the end of the school day, rather than heading straight home, they would go to the coconut plantation on the way. They had sticks hidden in various places on both sides of the road; they also had kids among them who were adept at climbing coconut trees. They would eat their fill of coconuts to the point where they could hardly walk the rest of the journey home.

There were some scary moments. Like the day Egya Amakyi, Ebela's former husband who over time had become rather mean and irritable, decided he had had enough of watching his coconuts get continually depleted by a bunch of hungry teenagers. It was a Wednesday afternoon. He put on a pair of old pants and wellington boots and set off for the farm, a large, sharpened cutlass in his hand. Aso wondered why her husband was leaving for the farm so late. She tried to convince him to stay at home since the sun was too hot for someone his age. Amakyi would have none of it. Of late he went there less often, having handed over the day-to-day work on the farm to his sons. However, he had not been impressed with how the younger men were handling the work, and the number of times he had heard passersby tell him of the havoc those unruly schoolchildren were wreaking on his coconuts. "Oh how things have changed," he lamented to whoever would listen. In his days, teenagers were busy learning to prepare themselves for life as fishermen or farmers. Boys learnt to sharpen their swimming skills, how to maintain the canoe and the nets, and what to look for when they went to guide a net filled with fish to the shore. The girls among them were settling down in their marital homes or preparing themselves for it. Now here were these teenagers, idling about in classrooms under the pretext of going to school, only to come out and descend on his coconut plantation. School, in his view, was for lazy children. He was glad none of his children had settled for such a life of idleness. Today, this Wednesday, he must exact his pound of flesh.

School closed at the regular time—two-thirty PM. As they had done countless times before, Bomo and her friends set off from the school premises in groups. They argued about anything— which teachers gave the meanest punishments at school, whether the latest catch by *Sea Never Dry* fishing group was the largest, and so on. Once they got to Egya Amakyi's sprawling coconut plantation they took a detour and walked noisily into the bush as usual, oblivious of the danger they were walking into. They scouted the area until they found just the right tree with enough fresh coconuts for all of them. They took out the two long raffia sticks they had hidden nearby and started poking at the fruits. That was when Eduku, a precocious boy who Bomo and her friends had nicknamed *Obrafuo* for always telling them how dangerous it was to be plucking the coconuts without the owner's consent, called out.

"Guys watch out! There comes Egya Amakyi!"

There he was, running towards them with all the strength of an angry eighty-year-old, brandishing his shiny cutlass in the air. They ran for dear life. It was the fastest run Bomo had undertaken. They were all able to outrun him. Bomo and the two kids closest to her hid in a bush and lay very still on the ground. She almost fainted when a millipede wriggled its way towards her, brushing her legs. The others quickly scattered and hid, two behind a small hill overtaken by shrubs, while the rest under the dried coconut branches on the ground. They were fortunate that Amakyi's eyesight was also beginning to fail. He stood around for what seemed like eternity to the frightened kids. Seeing that he had been outmanoeuvred by those "godforsaken kids," he cursed angrily, waved his cutlass in the air, and left. He took some of the husk from a coconut that had been eaten previously. The children concluded that he could be going to curse them with it.

Bomo and her friends hid in the bushes until they were sure he had gone away, then they came out and continued their journey home, debating whether he had seen any of them, knowing that if he had, their parents would be hearing of it very soon. That encounter kept them out of his plantation for about two weeks. Not even the fear of what Egya Amakyi may have done with the old coconut husk scared them into leaving his plantation alone.

There were also those days in the rainy season when the river became so full that Bomo and her friends had to remove all their clothes to be able to cross it and then dress up on the other side, before continuing their journey to or from school. On days like that it took a lot of dedication and commitment to go to school. Sometimes when the water level rose too high, it became scary. Two times the canoe taking them capsized and they had to swim ashore. Swimming was one of the most important life skills a child living in Aakonu could have. The first time the canoe capsized was when they were in Grade Seven. It had rained a lot during the night. It was examination time and they could not skip school. The examination at the end of each of the three terms in the academic year determined whether or not a pupil made it to the next class at the end of the year. In the schools in both Aakonu and Kamunu failing a class did not only mean they had to repeat, it was also very embarrassing. The last day of each term all parents were invited to the school. The pupils brought foodstuffs and drinks while the school purchased a sheep or chickens for the party. The money for it was usually from work the pupils did during the term. They hauled sand for those who needed it, did weeding and odd jobs under the supervision of the teachers, in order to raise the money for the end-of-term party. After the feast, the school bell rang for all pupils, parents, and teachers to congregate in one of the larger classrooms. There were no auditoriums at that level. Once everyone was seated quietly, the headteacher strode in with the examination results. The pupils would be called up by class. The headteacher would read out their names one by one based on how well they had done. The first ten pupils usually received a resounding applause. One by one they came up, shook the hand of the headteacher, and went to sit down. The applause died down as the last but fourth pupil was called.

The remaining three, in the words of the headteacher, were said to be carrying the stinky basket for the term. It was an unbearably embarrassing situation to find oneself in. That was why, even when the river was too high to cross, Bomo and her friends still tried to go to school. To them, the embarrassment of carrying the stinky basket trumped the fear of the high currents of the river.

Bomo: Dying for Nana

BOMO MISSED HER GRANDMOTHER. Nana had been a pillar in our lives for as long as she could remember, but like many other children, she got to know that Nana was not her biological grandmother only after she died. That made her even more unforgettable. Nana always made her feel special. She always had the right words to praise and encourage her when she did something good, and to correct her when she needed to be corrected. Even when Nana was mad at her she spoke in such a way that Bomo could hardly take offence. She wanted to please her Nana so much that it made me jealous sometimes. She went all out when she had to do anything for Nana. She did her best to please her because it felt natural to do so.

One day there was nothing to cook with at home. Bomo was eight years old. She was playing with her friends when one of them mentioned how much *enwone* people had caught the previous day. Enwone are like mussels but with a smooth shell. They tend to be a delicacy, but are quite easy to catch when in season. They burrow into the seabed, and to catch them people waded up to their knees and moved their feet around to dig into the soft bed. To strangers this might look as though they were dancing in the water. Bomo picked up a midsized bowl and followed her three friends Eduku, Akasi, and Akuba to the seashore. The tide had begun to rise, but they didn't give it a thought. True to what they had heard, there were a lot of enwone to catch. Within minutes her bowl was full.

She was so engrossed in what she was doing that she did not see a big wave gathering ahead. By the time she raised her head to look, it was too late. The wave was upon her and pushed her down, bowl and all, and she was at the bottom, rolled along by the wave as it receded. Her friends did not realize that she had fallen, until they were making for the shore when Eduku realized that Bomo was missing. He screamed, "Where is Bomo?"

They looked frantically for her but could not see her. The wave was taking her further out. Finally they spotted her, when the wave had receded. But there was an even bigger wave gathering. Eduku ran as fast as he could towards her and dove under the wave to grab her before she was pulled further. Akuba and Akasi helped to drag Bomo out of the water and to the shore. She was almost lifeless, having taken in so much water her stomach looked distended. Akuba ran out screaming for help. A few people heard them and ran over and began to resuscitate her. Once she was conscious they gave her something that caused her to throw up water. By this time word had reached Nana that Bomo had almost drowned in the sea. I had gone to the market, and Nana was beside herself.

Bomo: A Small Fish in a Big Pond

SOON IT WAS TIME FOR secondary school. Bomo did so well in the entrance exams that getting admitted was not an issue. Her issue was remembering the order of the three schools that she had indicated as her choices of places she might want to go to. She was the first in her family to make it this far. As for Uncle Mieza, there was no need to involve him.

The schools were competitive, and they prided themselves in the students they attracted. This meant that as soon as the entrance exam results were released, the schools would target and offer admission to those top students who had made them their first choice. They would then consider those who had picked them for their second choice. By the time Bomo and her mother visited the three schools on Bomo's list, the school that was her first choice had replaced her because she was too late in accepting their offer. Her second choice had her on their waiting list. In the end, she got enrolled in Western Secondary School in WestBay, the western regional capital. Unlike many of the top schools, Western Secondary did not have as many students and so Bomo was able to gain admission to it.

Finally the day came for her to travel to school. This was her first ever visit to a major city. WestBay was about two hundred kilometres southeast of Aakonu. It had a population of over one million residents. Bomo was both excited and nervous the day she left. Saying goodbye to her mother and Nana and her siblings Noba, Kane and Menyena, was the hardest part. By this time Noba and Kane had also started attending middle school in Kamunu. She felt especially concerned about them, knowing what she had just gone through. Menyena, on the other hand, was still too young. She was the only one of Bomo's siblings still at the local school.

Nana and Ahu gave Bomo a lot of advice, especially to be careful of bad company and bad influences, to stay focused and away from boys (parent talk for don't get yourself pregnant), and to be a good girl generally. Bomo was determined to follow these warnings. Although she was on a scholarship, it would still cost a considerable amount of money to get everything she needed for the boarding house.

On the day of the journey, Bomo got up very early, having hardly had any sleep. She had already started packing the week before. Some of the items she needed were not available in Aakonu, so she had to get them in WestBay. As there were no lorries that left directly from Aakonu her mother had to accompany her to Sanvoma. They stayed over at the lorry station in Sanvoma till about four the next morning when the first lorry for WestBay arrived at the station. The lorry, with the inscription ɔbayɛ boi—*It shall be well* was already overloaded, filled with traders and their goods. Baskets full of smoked fish, cassava, containers of coconut oil and luggage of regular travellers, including Bomo's airtight, were fully packed on top of the lorry. The driver's mate helped Bomo climb into the truck. She sat on one of the ten wooden planks between a nursing mother and a middle-aged man. As Ahu waved her daughter goodbye she wondered whether she was doing the right thing leaving her on her own at that early age. Fortunately, Gokeh's brother Blay, who lived in the city, had assured them that he would have someone at the lorry station in WestBay to help Bomo get to her school safely. That gave her some relief.

Meanwhile, after about two hours in the lorry Bomo had started to doze off when the driver's mate announced to all passengers to alight. They had reached a pontoon over the Ankobra river. It was early morning. The sight of the river entering the sea in the distance turned Bomo nostalgic. The passengers stood together on the pontoon as it moved gradually towards the other end of the road. Bomo could not believe what she was seeing.

Soon everyone was seated again and ɔbaye boɛ, the lorry, continued on its way. Before they could settle in their seats, a young man of about thirty, with a small bag on his shoulder and his right fist folded in front of his mouth like a microphone, stood up in the small space between the passengers and the driver. He asked everyone to bow their heads in prayer. The passengers obliged him without a question.

"Father God we thank you for this journey," he began. "We have come from different parts of this land. Please take us safely to our destinations. And the crowd said!" He paused waiting for the people to respond.

"Amen," came the enthusiastic chorus.

Now that he had everyone's attention, he cleared his throat, brought out a few small bottles of concoctions from his sachet and began:

"Who here suffers from high blood pressure?" He waited for a bit. No response.

"Dizziness?" A few people responded.

"What about sugar disease?" A few people raised their hands. "Hold it there," he instructed.

"Now anyone suffering from *dwinso mogya* (prostate cancer)?"

Two middle-aged men raised their hands.

"This medicine," he held up his bottles high enough for everyone to see. "It cures all of these diseases. You take this bottle, shake it, pour one tablespoon into your morning cup of porridge, mix, and drink it. You do this for a month and you would be free of all these ailments."

The man sold most of his medicine bottles and alighted at the next stop.

As they entered the city, Bomo could not believe her eyes. The roads were so wide lorries passed each other on both sides. They did not have to stop for others to pass them, as they did in Aakonu and even in Awiane. After stopping at a petrol station—which Bomo thought at first was the destination—the lorry finally stopped at the bus station. Bomo did not know where to go. There were people coming out from everywhere she looked. Traders with goods, young boys pushing trolleys, driver's mates calling out for passengers, workers dressed in formal clothes. People speaking various languages she did not understand. It was overwhelming. Bomo found a spot by a group of shops and put her luggage down. She sat on her airtight and put her sack with the little money and foodstuffs her mother had given her on her lap. She looked very lost.

A group of boys gathered on the opposite side of where she sat seemed to notice how green and lost she looked.

"Are you waiting for someone?" One of them walked to her

and asked in pidgin.

She pretended not to hear him and looked straight at nothing in particular.

"Hey, I am talking to you. Are you waiting for someone? This is not a waiting place."

Bomo looked up at him.

"Yes I am, and where is the waiting place then?" she asked.

"Who are you by the way?" she asked as an afterthought.

"My name is Ebo. I am here with my friends." He pointed to the group of boys.

"Here, let me help you." He offered.

Bomo obliged. Ebo helped Bomo carry her luggage and then offered to hold her sack so her hands would be free to hold the airtight she was carrying on her head. He led the way to where Bomo thought was the waiting area. Then it all happened so suddenly. He was walking so quickly, zig-zagging between the cars that Bomo could hardly keep up with her heavy luggage. Before she realized, the very helpful-looking Ebo was nowhere to be found. Her sack was gone, and with it the three hundred shillings pocket money and the food her mother had given her. Bomo was shaken. She did not know whom to tell. How could she know the next person she talked to wouldn't turn out to be like him?

She was still carrying her luggage, not knowing where to go when a young man of about twenty years tapped her on the shoulder.

"Are you Bomo?" He asked in her language.

Bomo was relieved to finally hear someone speaking her language in this strange place.

"Yes I am. Who are you?" she asked.

"My name is Papa Gokeh Junior. My father, Mr Blay, asked me to meet you at the lorry station and take you to your school.

I was waiting at the lorry station but your lorry was delayed so I decided to run to the shop to get a few items. When I returned I saw the lorry had arrived, but you were nowhere to be found."

Bomo could breathe easy now.

"Oh, okay. That makes sense now. But how did you find me since we have never met?" she queried.

"Uncle Gokeh gave my father a good description of you. It wasn't difficult to make you out. Moreover, not many people are walking around here carrying an airtight on their heads."

They both laughed.

Bomo did not tell him about her stolen sack.

The city was like nothing she had imagined. The wide roads, the big houses, cars moving in different directions. She wondered how people found their way in this vast place. What intrigued her the most was the sight of people moving in between the cars. She had seen only six cars come to Aakonu during her entire life. She saw a few more when she was with Uncle Mieza in Awiane. In Aakonu, when people heard a car coming, they ran away in different directions. Now here she was, with hundreds of cars one after another and people walking in between them like they did not care about their lives. Bomo had a lot of questions but she dared not ask, for fear of being called a villager. In the night she wondered about the lights that shone like little stars from the electric poles along the roads and in people's homes. How did they get there, and who cleaned them when the bulbs got dirty? She thought of the kerosene lanterns she used at home and how they needed to be cleaned of soot every evening. Even the water flowing from the taps intrigued her. In Aakonu she knew exactly where the water was coming from, the well or the river. Here she could not tell. All she did was turn the tap and water poured out of nowhere.

Bomo's first week at school was challenging. Everything was new and different. She could not speak in Nzema because nobody in her class could speak or understand it. All the students were required to speak English only. Bomo had been good at reading and writing English, but she had never been comfortable speaking it in Aakonu, for fear of being branded a show-off. She did not need to speak English at Awiane when she was staying with Uncle Mieza, because it was not a requirement, and all the students spoke and understood Nzema. Even Nicholas from the secondary school at Awiane, who brought Uncle Mieza's food, did not speak English with her. The few times he tried, Bomo was too shy to answer, and always found a way to defer to Uncle Mieza. Now she could not hide any more. The feeling of inadequacy almost eroded her self-confidence. And if that were not enough, a new friend she had made was bullied and beaten so badly that she had to be taken back home.

Her name was Yaba and she came from Bokabo. Bomo had met her when they sat at the same table for dinner the first week of school. At the boarding house, the girls stayed in two large girls' dormitories. The boys had three dormitories as there were more boys than girls. The students were assigned to six different houses, conveniently named by numbers. Each house had a male and a female prefect and assistant prefect. Each house had a housemaster for the boys and a housemistress for the girls. Yaba was assigned to House Six, while Bomo was in House Three.

Like Bomo, Yaba was the first in her family to make it this far in her education, and she felt equally lost. Unfortunately for her, House Six was notorious for having the most bullies in the school. Many junior students had to be taken under the protection of senior students. Poor Yaba had no protector. Few people wanted to be associated with a village girl. When one of the popular girls asked for her favourite t-shirt and she refused, she knew she was going to be in trouble. But she could not have imagined how bad it would be.

It was about six weeks after they had been in school. The entire school was preparing for the annual inter-colleges festival, a very competitive athletics festival between all the secondary schools in the western region. There were about twenty-four schools in all. The top three schools earned the bragging rights for being the best in athletics in the region. Not only that, the top athletes from each sport were picked to represent the region at the national level. From that point, the best were selected to represent the country at the Commonwealth and Olympic Games. In Western Secondary, preparations for the competition began at the start of the academic year in early September and went on until the last race had been run, in February the following year. During the first four weeks of September everyone went for the training. At dawn, at about five AM, the Athletics Prefects in the various dormitories rang the bell. The House Prefects mobilized their students for a five-kilometre jog, from the campus through the naval base to the WestBay beach and back to the school field for even more laps. These intense preparations culminated in the annual inter-house competitions in October. The best athletes were chosen to represent Western Secondary at the inter-colleges.

Early one Saturday morning, when the students returned from jogging, one of the girls shouted "Thief, thief!" and pointed at Yaba. Just like that, about eight students standing by Yaba started beating her up until one senior girl stood up, screamed at them, and threatened to call the police.

The House Six girls' prefect notified the house mistress, who brought the issue up with the headmaster and his team. The culprits were punished, but not too severely, and Yaba's family was notified. They came and took her away.

Once the shock of the initial days wore off, Bomo settled into the school routine. She poured her everything into her studies. She knew there would be no second chance for her if she failed to make the most of her time in school. There would be no extra classes or private tutorials for her if she failed any class. Even if there was money to pay, there were no such services available in Aakonu when she returned for vacations. But before long she was top of the class. And gradually she made a few friends. There were students from all walks of life, from different regions in the country. That was the beauty of being in the boarding house. Over time Bomo became more comfortable speaking in English. That did a lot to boost her self-confidence.

She looked forward to the end of school when she could go home to the village. Most of all she wanted to see Nana, who was advancing in age. She could already see the changes in her own generation. A number of her childhood friends were already married. People wondered out aloud whether spending so much time in school would not affect her ability to have children in the future. It did not bother her. To those who would listen she gave free advice about the importance of secondary education and opportunities for the future. She spoke of her experience of the city. And she became increasingly aware that she would have to stand up for herself when the pressure came to get married.

Something happened when she was in Form Four. She had returned to school after a tumultuous summer during which her uncle, Homiah's brother, Blay, who had been supporting her since she started schooling in the city, passed away. Not only that, just before school reopened her aunt Mua, Ahu's elder sister, also died suddenly. Bomo was devastated. She was concerned about leaving Nana and her mother Ahu to go back to school, not knowing whether they would be there when she returned.

Not long after Bomo returned to school, she received an urgent message from home. It was just after an English class. She had recently chosen her major and was settling in to a routine in the class. In Western Secondary, like many of the secondary schools in the country, all students took a list of core subjects—English, mathematics, general science, social sciences, religion and local languages. In addition there were a number of elective subjects that students could take. In Form Four, students chose their major in addition to the core subjects. Bomo chose science as her major, which was expected since she and her mother Ahu always believed she needed to be a doctor just like Dr Ama Boah at the clinic in Bokabo.

The teacher asked her to see him after the lesson.

"Bomo, the headmistress gave me a note for you. She says it was left at her office some time this morning."

It was a message from her mother asking her to come home as soon as she could.

Bomo was worried. Had there been another death in her family? Who could it be this time? Was her Nana all right? Her mother? She sought permission from school and left for Aakonu that weekend. She was immensely relieved when she reached home and saw both her mother and her Nana. As soon as she put her bag down she asked, "Maame what's wrong? What's so urgent that I had to come home in a rush? You got me worried."

Her mother reassured her, "My daughter Bomo, no, there is nothing wrong with anyone. We are all doing very well." She added, "You know how much I value your education, Bomo my daughter. But as you can see I can only earn enough to take care of your siblings and their schooling here in the village. Ever since you have been away in the big school, I have been relying on support from your uncle Blay. Now that he is no more, your Nana and I worried that we may not be able to support your schooling. Fortunately, a very prominent man from Sanvoma who is also an educator based in WestBay is looking to marry an Nzema girl who is educated. Imagine how convenient that would be. He has promised to make sure that you continue your schooling after the wedding. We thought it would be a good idea, because that will ensure that you do not drop out of school because of lack of money."

Bomo could not believe her ears. She was flabbergasted.

"Mother," this was the first time she had referred to her mother this way instead of "Maame."

"Is this why you sent me that urgent message? You had me so worried that something had gone wrong at home." Bomo pretended to be interested. "Who is this man? Has he married before? What happened to his wife?"

"His name is Egya Miah. He is about your stepfather Gokeh's age," Ahu replied. "I have not seen him personally, but the person who brought Nana the news did indicate that he looked younger for his age. You know what happens with those city folks. Even when they are old, they look younger than those of us who have been aged by hard work on the farm and at sea. He has never married before. From what I heard, he has been going to school his entire life. He has just recently realized that life is passing him by, hence his desire to find a wife," Ahu concluded, unsure whether she had been convincing enough.

"Maamee!" Bomo responded, intentionally stretching the last syllable. "How could you even think like that? There is no way I will marry a man old enough to be my father. Besides, for all you know this promise to help with my education may just be a ploy to marry me."

She was extremely disappointed. Her mother had been her role model. Now here she was, proposing to give her away to an old man.

"I am only trying to make sure you don't have to stop school," her mother said, sensing how disappointed she was. "Can you promise me you will do your best and stay in school no matter the financial challenges?"

Bomo smiled.

"Mother, you don't have to marry me off just because you don't have enough money to see me through school. I am determined to get through it no matter what. What I would not like is to get married at this age to anybody, whether they promise to take care of my schooling or not."

With that, Bomo returned to school. And her mother felt proud of her daughter. She told her kinsmen that her daughter didn't need to get married. They were not pleased. How could she side with an evidently foolish girl, who did not know what was good for her? How could she let such a good opportunity pass? What was the importance of so much schooling for a girl anyway? Instead of convincing Bomo to get married to an important man so that the whole family would benefit, she had sided with her in her waywardness. Her sons Kane and Noba would have benefited too, because Egya Miah would have taken care of their schooling as well. Bomo was being selfish.

Bomo returned to school with an even stronger resolve to complete her education. She did not want to overburden her mother with requests for money. She made full use of the dining hall, and got called names for that. Although three meals a day were included in the boarding fees, most girls, especially in the senior classes, preferred to skip them, because the food was considered of poor quality and girls who frequented the dining hall were considered "not cool." Girls from wealthy homes had enough food in their cubbies to feed them the entire school term, in addition to pocket money to buy food from outside.

Bomo endured the taunts and stayed resolved to study hard enough to ace her exams. Soon enough both her teachers and the other teachers in the school took notice. They began discussing her in the teachers' common room, wondering what record she was likely to set for the school during the final examinations. They were using Bomo as an example for their students, especially the juniors. That was how a junior student named Ekoa got to know about the petite, unassuming senior who was being tipped to set a record for the school during the Secondary School Certificate Examinations. That weekend when Ekoa went home, her father, a prominent retired army officer named Colonel Assuah, who was also a strong advocate for girls' education, wanted to know how things were going at his daughter's school. When Ekoa told him about Bomo, Colonel Assuah was so impressed he wanted to know more.

"Where is she? Who are her parents? What does she plan to do after secondary school?" he asked Ekoa.

"Papa," Ekoa said, "I know that she is from Aakonu. I do not know much about her family. One thing I do know is that she could do with some help. She does not look like she has a lot of money for her upkeep at school."

Colonel Assuah knew what he would do. He gave Ekoa a note to give to Bomo when she returned to school. It read:

Dear Bomo,

My name is Col. Assuah. My daughter, Ekoa, a student at your school, has told me a lot about you. I am very impressed with what you are doing, and would like to meet you.

I would like to meet your parents as well so you can be sure I do not have any ill intentions.

I look forward to meeting you soon.
Signed.
Col. Assuah

Bomo had mixed feelings when she got the message. On one hand she was flattered that her hard work at school had been acknowledged. At the same time, she was unsure whether the colonel's interest would not become something else. Nonetheless, when she went home for the end of term holidays, she told her mother about the colonel's invitation. Ahu did not miss a beat.

"My daughter," she told her, "if this man is who his daughter says he is, then you will have nothing to fear. Let us go and meet him. You will have time to decide what to do once we hear what he has to say."

On Saturday, one month after receiving his invitation, Bomo and her mother travelled to WestBay to meet Colonel Assuah. The journey took them almost a full day. They got there at around six PM. The elderly, medium-built man had the demeanor of an accomplished soldier. He lived on the third floor of a three-storey building in the middle of the city, one of three such buildings that he owned. A big family man, his home was full of people. His ten children, some older than Bomo and a few younger ones like Ekoa, were at different stages in their schooling. There were about fifteen other young people in his household that he was supporting in school as well.

"You are very welcome. Make yourselves comfortable," Colonel Assuah welcomed the two women heartily. Once they were seated, Ahu and Bomo introduced themselves and why they were there. Ahu explained that Bomo's father had passed away when she was young, and she, Ahu, was no longer with her stepfather. Her brother, Ahu's uncle, had been helping with her schooling but he had passed away recently. Currently, she was the key person taking care of Bomo's education. That was why it was only she who came with Bomo.

The colonel nodded. He had water brought for them. Then he went straight to the point, addressing Ahu.

"Ahu, I have heard a lot about your daughter, and the hard work she is doing at school. As you can see, I love it when I hear of girls who take school as seriously as your daughter is doing. You have done an excellent job with her. I called you here to let you know that I would be more than happy to take over all of her school expenses going forward. I do not know what your financial situation is, and whether or not you need the help. But if you do," he continued, "I am more than happy to step in. From now onwards, you do not have to worry about her. You can save whatever money you would spend on her, and use it for your other children."

Ahu was speechless, and so was Bomo. Ahu knelt to thank him for his kind gesture.

"Get up. You don't need to thank me. Give thanks to God. As the elders say, he who climbs a tree is the one that can be pushed. Your daughter is doing a good job and deserves the help she is getting." He held her hand to help her up.

"We need more girls educated. And a girl as clever as Bomo here deserves all the help we can give her." The two women thanked the colonel profusely.

"From now onwards, Bomo," he turned to her. "This is your home. You are always welcome here. After you see your mother off to Aakonu, if you would like to come to the city to continue your studies before school re-opens, you are welcome to do so. If you ever need anything, do not hesitate to inform me."

Bomo returned to Aakonu with her mother. She was very excited, and thankful that her money worries were over. "You see, Maame, I am going to be able to continue schooling without getting married."

To qualify and be able to attend a good college or university Bomo had to get excellent grades.

It was no surprise to anybody that when the results of the final external exams came, she was among the top ten percent in the entire country. And as expected, she had set a new record at Western Secondary as well. She was ecstatic. Colonel Assuah and his household could not hide how proud they were of her. Ahu's joy knew no bound. As for Bomo, the sky was her limit now.

Soon she got the confirmation that she had been accepted to complete the two-year pre-university program at SouthWestern Academy, also in WestBay. Most secondary schools, including Western Secondary and SouthWestern Academy followed the regular five years secondary and two years post-secondary system. Bomo could have completed the two years post-secondary program at Western. However, she felt that doing the two years at a different school would help expand her network. Her first day at SouthWestern was way different from that at Western Secondary. The colonel made sure she had what she needed to be comfortable at school.

Gone was the scared, lost girl who had entered Western Secondary a few years earlier. In her place was a confident young woman, ready to make the most of what this new opportunity had in store.

Bomo: Finding Love

WHILE SHE WAS HOME WAITING for school to reopen Bomo usually helped her mother at the eatery. On market days she would go to the market in NewTown to buy groceries for it. During one such visit, she met Eti, a young man from Aakonu who was doing his postsecondary national service, having just completed his two year pre-university program, the sixth form. All students in the country were expected to complete two years of national service, one year after completing secondary school and the next one after completing studies at a tertiary institution.

He was teaching at the secondary school at Awiane for his national service, the same school where Uncle Mieza had taught earlier. He was one of the few boys from Aakonu to have made it this far beyond middle school, and one of two who were on track to attend university. He had heard of Bomo's performance in her secondary school exams, bragged about her at his school, and was hoping to see her the next time he visited Aakonu. Eti was as outgoing as Bomo was shy. He was in his early twenties and of athletic build, a very self-confident young man who did not let his humble beginnings take away from who he was and what he aspired to be. Eti knew even in primary school that he wanted to be a diplomat, someone working for a large international organization, moving from country to country.

Bomo recalled meeting him a few years earlier. She had just started middle school then and he was in his first year at the secondary school. Still a wide-eyed young girl, she had heard a phrase from school that said "better be late than the late." She had heard that this young man was very smart and was impressed by his confidence with speaking English, given her own reluctance to speak it, out of fear of making a mistake or being labeled a "know-it-all."

Bomo had run up to him and asked, "What does it mean when someone says 'better be late than the late'?"

He gave her a hard look that seemed to say, "How dare you?"

Scared by his reaction, Bomo had run home without waiting for a response. Now eight years later they were meeting at the marketplace. The change in his attitude, his sudden civility surprised her. He could have forgotten that first episode, but for her it was as fresh as though it had happened yesterday. When he invited her to have lunch with him, she said yes, curious to find out what had changed since the last time. Bomo was in for a greater surprise. Eti took her to one of the best eateries in NewTown. He was the perfect gentleman, and they sat down to a meal of rice balls in peanut butter soup. He wanted to know what she had been up to, whether she had enjoyed her time at school, congratulated her on her excellent grades, and what her plans were for the future. Bomo was on her guard all the while, expecting him to boil over at any moment. To her amazement, he continued to be as charming as ever, telling her what he had been up to and how impressed he was by her. They discussed what it was like to grow up in a small village like Aakonu, and be the first in their families to make it as far as they had done.

"So, what are you planning to do with these wonderful grades?" Eti asked her.

"Well, I would like to continue to the sixth form and then go to university, and then take it from there," she answered, flattered by his question.

"That is excellent. I would like us to do this again. I will come by to see you, when I visit home next week."

They said goodbye and parted company. On her way back to the village, Bomo wondered all the while about Eti's changed attitude towards her.

The following Saturday late afternoon, while Bomo was pounding fufu in front of the kitchen, Eti came to visit. He greeted Bomo and her mother, who offered him a seat. It was then that Bomo remembered that he had said he would be coming to the village that weekend. He said that he had come to visit his family and wanted to pass by to say hello. Bomo's mother was extremely surprised by this visit, of which she had had no inkling. She had known Eti since he was a young boy. She told Bomo to get the guest a glass of water to drink. After a few minutes of conversation, Eti sought permission to leave and Bomo saw him off.

There is a proverb that says "What an elder sees sitting down, a child can not see even if he stood on a long pole." Bomo's mother had already deduced that there was something more to Eti's impromptu visit to her compound than a mere hello to a middle-aged woman he had never said hello to before, let alone visited.

As soon as they were outside, Eti whispered to Bomo to meet him at the beach that evening, and then they said goodbye. Bomo came back to resume pounding the fufu.

◈

Ahu

I did not mention to Bomo how curious I was about Eti's visit. She might have thought I would want to know what they talked about while she saw him off but I said nothing. As she had come to realize, I could be impossible to read sometimes. One time I am very curious, wanting to know everything my daughter had been up to. Other days I just couldn't be bothered. Bomo still wasn't sure which Ahu she liked more. Although she sometimes pretended to dislike my nosiness, I knew she appreciated the fact that her mother cared enough to want to know in the first place. I was like a big sister to her. In fact people who did not know us usually mistook us for siblings—I was in my teens when I had her. People could see this in the way we interacted with each other. Bomo could discuss anything with me—boys, school, and issues with friends. This was unusual, given that most girls in the village were so afraid of their parents. Children were not expected to question or talk back to their elders.

My daughter would speak her mind and ask me questions. She would object if something did not make sense to her. Even at a young age she had wondered why many girls were not in school. Why were most families keeping their girls at home and only sending boys to school? Why was she expected to do house chores and not her brothers? Why was it that only women were often called witches and accused of causing harm to children? Why would a woman care for a child until it was grown enough to be able to take care of her, and then decide to use witchcraft to kill it? Some of these questions were beyond me. I wondered sometimes whether the gods gave Bomo to me as payback for my own nonconforming behaviour.

Rather than shut her down, I would tell her the truth if I did not have an answer, "Bomo, I do not know why. You will understand when you grow up."

Bomo

Bomo finished her chores around seven that evening. It was already dark in the village, and lanterns had been lit in the compounds. Bomo told her mother she was meeting Eti by the beach, close to the village square.

"Bomo, be very careful. You know what I have always said. This is not the time to get yourself into any trouble with a pregnancy you are not ready for."

"I will be careful, Maame," she replied and ran off to the agreed spot before her mother could say another word. Eti was already waiting when she arrived.

"I am glad you came," he said. "I thought maybe you had changed your mind."

"No. Why would you think that? You know I had to finish what I had to do. Unlike you, I actually have chores to complete," she joked.

Eti looked at her. "Come closer. Are you scared of me?"

"No," she replied. "But I can hear you just fine."

"Then." He paused, then began. "Bomo, I have been meaning to tell you this for some time now. I have been thinking about what is next for me, and who I would like to continue with in the next chapter of my life. It's you. Bomo, I think I am in love with you. Since we met at the market place last week, I haven't been able to take you out of my mind. I see us making a future together, I wanted to let you know that."

Bomo was speechless. She liked what Eti said. What was there not to like? He was one of only a few young men in Aakonu who had gone far in his education. By all accounts he had a good future ahead of him. But could she trust him? What if he was saying all this only to deceive her? What would she do if she accepted his proposal and ended up pregnant before she had been able to get to where she would want to be?

"What do you have to say, Bomo?"

"Well, I like you too," she said, suddenly shy. "But how do I know you are not just saying this to trap me? I have to focus on my education, and getting entangled with a boy is not something that I would like to do."

Eti was not one to give up easily.

"You know I would not do such a thing. This is such a small village. If I did anything like that nobody would forgive me. Besides, I love you too much to destroy your future in any way."

Disarmed by how genuine he sounded, Bomo accepted his proposal, on condition that they would not start a sexual relationship. They would take time to study and help each other grow until they were both ready. At that point Eti would ask for her hand in marriage and then they would be able to do whatever they needed to do. She was surprised when he accepted her suggestion.

Elated that they had come to an agreement, Eti walked her home and returned to his house, feeling good about himself. He had no doubt that he had made a good "catch." Did he really like Bomo or was he using her as insurance? Many young men did that, especially when mother and grandma were on their case. Even when they were not ready, they would find a girl their pushy parents or grandparents would approve of, as if to say, here you are, and then go off to do whatever it was they were doing.

In his case, Eti himself had thought very seriously about who he wanted to settle down with, and Bomo was just the girl. He had dated a few other girls. There was a girl he had met in secondary school. Helena was wonderful, daughter of a teacher, and their relationship had started as a study partnership. He knew how much trouble he would be in if her father found out about them. That, however, did not deter them, they were so much in love, and they were already making plans for after school. It was a blow when after secondary school she was pressured into marrying someone else. They had thought they would take time for further studies, then marry when they were ready. But when a well-employed man came around and asked for her hand in marriage, the family accepted readily. She gave in and Eti was heartbroken. There were a few flings after that, but nothing serious. Now he couldn't think of anyone better than Bomo, and her acceptance meant a lot to him.

Bomo spent the entire night thinking about Eti's proposal and her response. What if he did not stick with their agreement? Had she got herself into a situation she would not be able to get out of? Convinced that they would not both be able to stick to their agreement, she wrote a note to Eti, rescinding her decision. To her disappointment, when she went to Eti's compound early the next morning, letter in hand, she found that he had already left. She walked down to the river's edge, hoping that he might be waiting there for the canoe. He wasn't there and she went back home.

Eti went on to continue his education at Empire University in Bay Coast while Bomo completed her two year pre-university program at SouthWestern Academy in WestBay. They continued to visit each other, and they got married just before Bomo entered Jubilee University in Nkran, the national capital. Eti was in his final year then, and he used part of his student allowance to support her family. When they went home during school holidays people marveled at seeing the two of them together. Two young people from the village who had chosen each other and still supported each other while educating themselves.

In Aakonu people began to think differently about marrying off their daughters. The girls saw in Bomo how important it was to go to university and not limit themselves to only the village school. They did not always have to accept whatever man was chosen for them by their parents, and it was important for them to reach their full potential.

Bomo: When life throws a wrench

ETI FINISHED HIS PROGRAM AND found a job teaching at a secondary school in Eshiem, some forty kilometres west of Aakonu. Whenever Bomo, who was still at university, came to visit, they lived in his unit at the teachers' quarters at the school. It was their home. Kane and Noba, Bomo's brothers, attended the same school and lived with them. During Bomo's third year at Jubilee University, the professors there went on strike. All the students had to go home. After almost a year, when the students were called back, she found that she was pregnant. What should she do? How would she combine being pregnant and studying at university? Should she abort? *Abortion?*

When she was in secondary school a tragic incident happened. It was a Thursday afternoon, she would always recall. They had come out of the dining hall and were on their way to their dormitories for a break when the news broke. A girl she knew had died. She was a brilliant student and she had gotten pregnant after having sex with a schoolmate. Carrying a pregnancy through the school term was impossible, she would be expelled; her parents would reject her. She saw abortion as her only way out. This was illegal, and so she went to see a quack, who gave her all sorts of concoctions that ended up killing her. It was an event that was strongly embedded in Bomo's mind.

She was determined, she would do no such thing. In the first place, she was a married woman with a caring husband. She was at university, where adult students did whatever they chose so long as it was not illegal. One only had to keep up one's grades and stay focused. A child at this stage did not fit into her and Eti's plans, but she would reach her goal regardless.

Eti was by her side every weekend and would always go with her to her appointments. Her roommates were on hand to advise. She had a friend who was like a mother to her on campus. Her Maame would come to visit regularly, bringing food and advice. Her gynecologist at the main teaching hospital was one of the best in the country. When it was time to have her baby she had all the help she needed. She had her baby girl, Yaba, the Thursday before her final exams on Monday. No special accommodation was made for her, and she sat through her exams like any other student. It was her best performance in all of her six years at Jubilee University.

And so she completed university with not only a degree, but also a husband and daughter, a picture of pride and accomplishment in her graduation photo, a degree in one hand and her daughter in the other. In her head, she could already see Dr Ama Boah of the clinic in Bokabo, passing the baton over to her.

Her husband Eti and her mother and siblings could not have been prouder.

Ahu:

As I stood beside my daughter, granddaughter in one hand and her degree in the other, I could not help but remember that late morning in the raffia and thatch makeshift bathroom, and the resulting miracle that changed my perspective on what a woman's life ought to be. I thought of the mother I never met, and Nana, Ebela, Aso, and Dr Ama Boah, the young doctor at the clinic. I see in my daughter Bomo today all the daughters of the village who would now dream of more than just preparing themselves to be given out in marriage.

Bomo: Epilogue

AS BOMO WATCHES HER OWN daughters grow from children to young adults, she is reminded of the strength of the girl child, from her own Nana to her mother, Ahu, and herself. She sees them overcome not only forced marriages to elderly men but also a system that sees their colour before it sees them. They may not have to worry about whether to go to school or not. Rather, they have to deal with whether their education has prepared them well enough for an ever-changing workplace. They do not have to navigate superstition and unwritten rules that hold down the girl child. Rather, they have to navigate a world that is constantly becoming a them-versus-us divide. They may not have to cross a river in a canoe to get to school. Rather they have to worry whether the school gates are secure enough against a shooter.

Is she scared? Sometimes. Is she worried? No. She has seen the girl child rise above it all. In the selflessness of her Nana, the resilience of her mother, and her own strong-mindedness, she sees her daughters triumph over it all. She sees the unbreakable spirit of the girl child. Like Nana, like Maame, like child, like grandchildren.

Elizabeth Allua Vaah hails from Bakanta, a small village on the western coast of Ghana, West Africa. She was the first in her family to attend high school and one of the first few girls in her village to go to university. *Maame* is Allua's first work of fiction.

Allua is an advocate for better maternal health through her foundation, the Vaah Junior Foundation. She is a strong advocate for girl child education, never failing to use her own life story as an example of how girls' education impacts generations. Allua lives in Canada with her family and works as a Risk Manager at a major bank in the Greater Toronto Area.